Stephen Buckley

SURFING
on a
CLOUD

authorHOUSE®

AuthorHouse™ UK
1663 Liberty Drive
Bloomington, IN 47403 USA
www.authorhouse.co.uk
Phone: 0800.197.4150

Published by AuthorHouse 11/08/2016

ISBN: 978-1-5246-3156-7 (sc)
ISBN: 978-1-5246-3157-4 (hc)
ISBN: 978-1-5246-3155-0 (e)

CHAPTER 1

Getaway

On a rainy Sunday morning, at the home he shared with his mother, Judith, Daniel Reed stumbled his way out of bed. Feeling hungover, he made his way to the kitchen in a desperate search for painkillers; his mum sang along to the radio, cooking a full English breakfast in an attempt to make her son feel better. Yesterday was his twenty-fifth birthday; he inherited nearly £700,000 from his late father's estate. This should have been a day for celebration. Instead, he spent the night alone, with nothing more for company than a bottle of vodka, drowning his sorrows. His girlfriend of seven years, Emma, had just told him she was pregnant with his child; this came as a complete surprise to him, especially when they'd made plans to travel the world together after he received his inheritance. He was even more surprised when she confessed to having an affair with his best friend, Jamie. He was heartbroken that the two people closest to him could have been so deceitful. He'd always feared that one day Emma would turn her attentions to him; he felt inferior to Jamie, who was a fitness fanatic and personal trainer. Daniel, on the other hand, was four stones overweight, drank heavily, and smoked, although he was equally good looking.

Emma had told him that Jamie was moving in with her. She blamed her newfound relationship on Daniel's immaturity and not giving a full commitment to their relationship – one of the factors being he still lived

1

with his mother. Daniel was comfortable living with Judith; they were more like flatmates than mother and son. They had become close after the death of his father six years earlier. Daniel loved Emma but wanted to see the world before settling down and having children. At only twenty-five, he didn't think he was being unreasonable.

Over breakfast, Judith could hear the hurt in her son's voice as he discussed the prospect of becoming a father. She knew it was not what he really wanted; well, not just yet. He was trying to put a brave face on it; he looked lost, like a child at his first day at school. He'd never been without a girlfriend or best friend. Judith blamed herself; maybe if she hadn't made him so comfortable at home, they might be living with her now.

As an attempt to cheer him up, she suggested they "do a little retail therapy, spend some of that tight old bastard's precious money," as she jokingly put it. Daniel smiled; he didn't need to be asked twice. He loved extravagant spending. In fact, the inheritance money couldn't have come at a better time. He was deeply in debt. His measly wage working at a supermarket distribution centre only just covered his monthly outgoings on credit cards and car finance.

Judith drove them to the Trafford Centre Shopping Mall in Manchester in Daniel's two-year-old BMW; after last night's drinking, he was in no fit state to drive. There they split up, arranging to meet at Starbucks at two o'clock. As much as they got on well together, Daniel didn't have the patience to follow her around endless clothes shops.

Judith arrived late at their arranged rendezvous. Her heart was filled with joy when she saw Daniel sitting surrounded by shopping bags; he looked happy and content. He told Judith he'd shopped for items he'd need for travelling. He'd just booked a first-class open return ticket to Bangkok, leaving tomorrow.

Judith forced herself to smile at his plans; inside, her heart was breaking. She knew she needed to be strong and support his plan, even though she knew this decision was purely to spite Emma.

Later that afternoon, he took a taxi to Emma's rented home in nearby Rochdale to let her know he was leaving. In his mind, he hoped for a reconciliation, wishing she'd rethink her decision and leave with him tomorrow for Bangkok.

"It's not too late," he said. "You could still come with me. I know this fling with Jamie won't last; you know it too."

"Perhaps you're right," she replied, "and yes, I'd love to come with you, but I know I'll never be enough for you. I know you want more than I can give. Danny, I know about your special relationship with Ross; he's my cousin, and he's never liked me. Seriously, did you think he was never going to tell? He took great pleasure in informing me that he was screwing my boyfriend."

"I'm sorry, so sorry, he was nothing more than an experiment. Is this why you chose Jamie, to hurt me?"

"No, I'd never do that," she said. "Perhaps Jamie's my experiment? I came to terms with you and Ross a while back. It's your lies I can't live with; you've never opened up to me! I know you used to hurt yourself, especially after your dad died. I know you used to cut yourself!"

He broke down into tears; she sat him down on the sofa and put her arms around him. She'd never seen this side of him before.

"I don't want to go," he cried. "I want to stay here with you!"

"No, Danny, you need to go; you need to find what you're looking for. See the world, have an adventure. You could meet the girl, or even the boy, of your dreams." She reached for his hand and placed it over her stomach. "In seven months' time, I'll be starting an adventure of a lifetime. I want this baby so much, and I want you to be around when he or she is born. I want you to be part of your child's life; you'll make a good father. But for now, you go, have a fantastic time, and make me jealous. You have the money to do it now!"

She kissed him goodbye and wished him good luck on his travels, although, deep in her heart, she wished she was going with him. Not knowing how long he'd be away for, he gave her enough money for twelve months' rent. They agreed to contact each other only in emergencies, hoping this would help them stay focused on their new lives apart.

Judith and his uncle Hugo took him to the airport the next day. Hugo was the brother of Daniel's late father; he had been like a father to him even before Graham died. Judith was a blubbering mess as she waved goodbye to him at the departure gates; she was worried sick about her son being alone in a foreign country. Hugo was there to comfort her in his arms, as he had done so many times before. Unlike Judith, Hugo knew a little more about his nephew; he believed he was more than capable of looking out for himself.

In New York City, Dr. Billy Frazier Fisher leaned against his desk at the Messier Global Shipping Building, looking with anger and disapproval at his son, Harrison, who was snorting cocaine from the arm of a leather sofa. Billy opened the top drawer of the desk and took out a roll of $50 bills and a gun. He walked over to his son and passed them to him.

"Here," he said sharply, "do us all a favour and buy as much white shit as you need to blow your brains out."

Harrison replied, whilst wiping his nose, "Carlos sends his regards, sir."

Billy was now enraged and furious; he grabbed Harrison by the collar and pulled him from out of the sofa, snarling, "You come here asking for more money and have the nerve to mention that punk's name in my company?"

"Sir, I need the money for a vacation. I'm leaving for Thailand in the morning with Ryan and Lucas."

Billy was happy with the prospect of his son leaving New York; it wouldn't do him any harm to get away from the temptations of the city, escaping from the grip of his drug dealers.

He calmed his temper and asked, "And how's it going with Susan?"

"Okay for now; she wants to travel Europe, but I'm not keen on that."

"You need to spoil her. Give her a big wedding; she'll soon forget Europe. You have your vacation, get yourself clean, come home, and make me a proud grandpa. So help me, Harrison, if you bring shame on this family, you'll end up a junky face down in the gutter, cut off, without a dime! You hear me?"

"Yes, I hear you, sir!"

CHAPTER 2

Bangkok

Daniel checked into the five-star Presidential Palace in downtown Bangkok at 9 a.m. Tuesday, 3 March. The hotel was more stunning than he imagined. He'd only ever stayed in a self-catering accommodation with Jamie in the Balearic Isles; his only other holidays were with his parents, staying at Hugo's villa in Tampa, Florida. After unpacking, he weighed himself; he'd recently been on a strict low-carb diet. He was now more determined than ever to lose weight.

He was in no rush to venture out of the hotel to explore; after a nap, he set up his new MacBook Air he'd bought on his shopping trip with his mum. He'd also bought an iPad and iPhone for Judith, to make video calls to her whilst he was overseas. He and Emma had agreed they wouldn't contact each other while he was away, but Daniel knew she'd be monitoring his whereabouts through Facebook. Before dinner, he walked around the hotel, taking photos, ready to post on line when he returned to his room later.

He'd decided to eat at the hotel's French restaurant, partly because he'd spotted the maître de earlier; she was stunning. In fact, she was the most beautiful girl he'd ever seen. She led him to his table like a model walking the catwalk. He was fixated by her beauty; once the menu was handed to him, it was only then he realised it was in French. With a helpful smile, she translated every dish; he couldn't take his eyes off her: her beautiful lips, perfect face, and pure porcelain skin. There was no doubt in his mind that if there were any truth about love at first sight, this was the moment.

After dinner, they chatted at his table. He made up a story that he was here mixing business with pleasure; he said he was searching for property to develop for his uncle's development company. She said her name was May and invited him to chat later when she waitressed in the piano bar.

Later, however, Daniel became frustrated, because the only free time she had, she spent talking to a stylish young French guy. She joked with him in fluent French.

He must be her boyfriend, he thought.

At one point, May and the French guy looked over at Daniel drinking his wine; they appeared to be talking about him in French. Daniel felt insecure; he was convinced she was telling him that he'd been flirting with her. May made her way over to Daniel, using the excuse that she was cleaning the table. She then asked a favour from him. The French guy's name was Auguste; he was on a five-day stopover in Bangkok before flying to Sydney. His partner, Christian, had recently been killed in a car crash, and May had taken pity on him. The stress of his recent bereavement had destroyed his confidence, and he had confined himself to the safety of the hotel since arriving three days ago, unable to face the busy streets of Bangkok on his own. May asked if Daniel could befriend him; she thought they could both benefit from each other's company. Daniel was relieved he was not her boyfriend; without a second thought, he immediately agreed. He'd have done anything for her.

Daniel walked over to Auguste's table and introduced himself; neither was particularly taken by formal pleasantries. Daniel ordered more wine, and they both bonded as they drank. Auguste was amused by Daniel's British sense of humour, and Daniel was impressed by his sense of style and sophistication, something Daniel could only aspire to.

Over the next two days, they were inseparable; they did the usual tourist attractions together. On the evening before Auguste's flight to

Australia, they were both tired and could not be bothered to dress for dinner. They drank wine and talked in the hotel lobby bar, both intrigued by each other's stories. The more Auguste drank, the more sombre his mood became; the conversation came to a standstill. Auguste's eyes were filled with sadness. Daniel asked if he'd like to talk about Christian.

"You're the first person I've spoken to about this, Daniel," he said. "On the night Christian died, I was with another man. Christian had become depressed over recent years; his family and I had tried everything to help. The more we tried, the more he pushed us away. On the night he died, I switched my phone off and went out looking for company. Christian was working away in Lyon. He'd often drink heavy on his own and call me to say he'd be better off dead! That night, I needed company; it's amazing how lonely you can become, even in a relationship. It was the first time in our ten-year relationship I cheated on him. Christian's car was found the next morning, overturned in a ditch, eighty kilometres from Toulouse. There were no witnesses to the accident and no alcohol found in his blood. I can only assume he was travelling home, concerned about me; however, the police were convinced it was suicide. You see, Daniel, whatever the truth, I will always carry the guilt of being responsible for his death."

Daniel moved around where Auguste was sitting to comfort his new friend. Auguste's story was not unlike Daniel's; he felt it was the right moment to share his own story of guilt and also thought he'd mention Ross in an attempt to cheer him up.

"At the time of my father's death, I also felt responsible. It was me that triggered his heart attack. The truth is, at nineteen, I wanted to rebel against everything, even my girlfriend. I wanted to do drugs and experiment with sex with another guy. I guess you could call me bisexual, although I do prefer women. A night out in Manchester's gay village led me to an evening of gay sex and drugs with my girlfriend's cousin, Ross. He worked on the doors of seedy bars and clubs. I must admit I jumped in at the deep end with my first gay sex experience. Ross was fixated by bondage; he was submissive and wanted to be disciplined with pain. That's where I came into the scenario. We'd often take our discipline sessions on location; he liked being punished in industrial settings, like old factories and disused warehouses, preferable where we stood a chance of being caught in the act. This added to our pleasure. One Sunday, we met at an empty warehouse near where I worked at the time. I knew the warehouse had a security guard who would often patrol inside. That day, I'd tied Ross naked to some storage shelf racking; with a whip in hand, I set to work on making Ross moan in ecstasy, hoping for the security guard to discover us, only it wasn't the security guard, it was my father!

"My phone was also switched off that day. I was using one of my father's company cars; unknown to me, the car was fitted with a tracking device. Because he couldn't contact me, he was worried, so he tracked the car's position. That's how he found us.

"He didn't speak, he just looked in disbelief and horror; speechless, he turned and ran back to his car. I quickly got dressed and followed. I followed him home; there in the driveway, he just sat in his car. Ross is mixed-race, and Father shouted racist, homophobic abuse at me from his car. I'd never seen him so angry; he even suggested I'd set the whole thing up for him to catch us, thinking I wanted to disgrace him.

"I guess I just snapped. I told him something he wasn't aware of: that his brother Hugo was in a relationship with a young black man, Jason. He knew Hugo was gay, but this subject was never mentioned in his company; he was mortified!

"It was then I suddenly remembered I'd left Ross tied up. I rushed back, dreading what condition he'd be in. I needn't have worried; he told me that hour he'd been tied up whilst I was away had been the most pleasurable experience of his life!

"I returned home to face Father's anger again; my mum had arrived home. She was in tears in the driveway, with my father's lifeless body still in his car; he'd suffered a fatal heart attack. Up until now, I've only told this story to my uncle. I was crippled with guilt. He reassured me my father had health problems; he was a ticking time bomb. Unfortunately, a heart attack was inevitable. My mother and I never knew this; we hardly saw him. He was bigoted alcoholic who was always working. You see, Auguste, my point is, you're still hurting, and you're punishing yourself with guilt. I punished myself after his death. I can assure you, it won't last forever."

Auguste walked over to Daniel and put his hand on his shoulder, thanking him for his thought-provoking story. Daniel suggested calling room service so they could eat together in their room and drink more wine. Auguste smiled and politely declined his offer. He made an excuse to leave, saying he must sleep in preparation for his long flight tomorrow. Daniel worried that he'd upset him.

At ten the next morning, they met in reception, waiting for Auguste's car to the airport. Auguste ordered Bucks Fizz to toast their brief friendship. Daniel asked why he left so soon last night; he didn't want it to distort their friendship.

"I wanted us to eat together and drink more wine," he said. "After that, I wanted to make love to you, Daniel! I'm not sure if you were aware of the signals you were sending me. Those two days we spent together made me happy at a time when I really needed to be happy. You have a kind heart, you're attractive, and you're wise beyond your years. You see, my heart is already breaking. I couldn't handle rejection from you at this moment. I see you have eyes for May."

Daniel, puzzled by this, apologised for giving him the signals; he joked he was completely unaware and flattered by his compliment. Although he thought maybe he'd slightly over dramatised the situation. *Perhaps it's a French thing,* he thought.

Just before his car arrived, they exchanged email addresses, promising to stay in touch. As the bellboy placed Auguste's luggage in the boot, instead of the customary European kiss on both cheeks, Auguste kissed him fully on the lips. It was a heartfelt kiss, with genuine affection. As he waved goodbye; Daniel felt sad; he'd miss his new friend. He felt more emotion for Auguste after two short days than he did after knowing Jamie after ten years. As much as he'd miss him, he knew that now he could concentrate on May.

Daniel spent most of that day working out at the hotel gym; he was still on a high after Auguste's flattering comments. His confidence was on an all-time high; he'd never thought of himself as attractive before. After the gym, he booked a table at the French restaurant; with this newfound confidence, he hoped he'd have the courage to ask May for a date. He made a special effort that evening; he squeezed into his newly bought Hugo Boss clothes. He was on a mission to impress.

That evening, as May walked him to his table, his nerves got the better of him. He was lost for words; all the seductive lines he'd planned to say had slipped from his head. However, he needn't have worried; as she brought over the menu, she whispered into his ear and asked him if he was free to spend tomorrow afternoon with her.

Daniel was tongue-tied. She smiled at his shocked expression and explained that Auguste had spoken to her. He'd complimented him for being such good company and a fine young gentleman. He'd also told her of Daniel's infatuation with her. Daniel couldn't believe his luck; he said a little prayer, thanking Auguste. Then he agreed to meet May the next day and turned his attention to his meal.

Later that night, he sent an email to Auguste, thanking him for his kind words.

Auguste replied affectionately:

> "No need, my friend, I speak the truth; you just be yourself
> with her and be truthful.
> We will meet again.
>
> Regards,
> Auguste"

The next day at noon, Daniel sat patiently in anticipation at the coffee bar next to the hotel; he spotted May from afar. He hardly recognised her at first; she was wearing denim shorts, a vest, and a loose silk shirt falling from her shoulders and tied around her tiny waist. She had on large black sunglasses, and her long black hair flowed wildly; her look was a contrast to how she dressed for work, where she'd wear a suit, full make-up, and her hair neatly tied back. She entered the coffee bar went outside to where Daniel was sitting. She lifted her glasses above her forehead to hold her hair back. Daniel stood when she approached his table, and she greeted him with a kiss. She took a seat as Daniel went inside to order coffees; when he returned, she was lighting a cigarette.

She asked, "I hope you don't mind?"

"Not at all," he replied as he lit his own, relieved that she also smoked.

After they finished their coffee, they took a tuk tuk to a riverside restaurant known for its finest Thai cuisine. May had always wanted to visit but had never had the money for such an extravagance. Over lunch, she looked puzzled at how little Daniel was eating. He told her he was dieting; she told him he was being ridiculous and flirtatiously said he looked perfect just as he is. After lunch, they took a river taxi to Damnoen Saduak Floating Market, where they boarded a longtail boat for sightseeing. Sitting close to each other, their bodies touched. Daniel put his arm around her shoulder, pulling her closer to his body. The floating market was fascinating, but did not interest either of them; their interest was firmly on their bodies touching. They would have preferred to get a hotel room together but held back for the temptation (well, for now).

They turned to each other with an uncontrollable desire to kiss, rocking from side to side in the tiny narrow boat; their lips eventually touched, only to be thrust forward as the boat came to an abrupt stop against the side. Both climbed from the boat, laughing hysterically. Their eyes met again, and the laughing stopped; they once again kissed passionately. They stood on a crowded, narrow step, being pushed and knocked about by the other tourists; this didn't interrupt them.

The next destination for the date was the Sky Bar, on the roof of the Labua State Building. Daniel had looked it up online last night and thought it was sure to impress her. A rooftop bar sixty-three floors high, and the views over Bangkok were breathtaking. May had heard of the Sky Bar but could only dream of visiting here. The cost of drinks was astronomical, but with Daniel wanting to impress her, no expense was spared. He ordered Champagne to sip whilst watching the sunset. Even though May was casually dressed, she was not out her depth at this extravagant rooftop venue; her style and sophistication were a sight to behold.

Daniel told her how about his relationship with Emma and how it ended; he also told her about the baby, insisting they would still continue being friends for the baby's sake. He didn't tell her about his inheritance; instead, he claimed he worked for his uncle Hugo, buying and renovating property around the world.

May lived with her mother and uncle in Don Sak, near the island of Koi Samui, where her mother managed the bar at a beach resort. To Daniel's surprise, May was told him she was born in Derby, England, which was only eighty miles away from his home in Manchester. Thomas, her father, was British; when their relationship failed, her mother and she moved back to Thailand. She's never seen her father since she returned to Thailand; over the years, she stayed in contact with him through email, and her mother often wrote to him, too. He helped her mother financially by buying her a house and contributing to May's education fees at university, where she was studying language. Already speaking fluent French and Spanish, she was also studying Arabic. She eventually hoped to teach in Europe, United Arabic Emirates, or Egypt.

After the Champagne bottle was empty, they drank cocktails, sitting close to each and other looking out onto the magnificent view. Around nine o'clock, May made her apologies, insisting she needed to return to her student accommodation. She needed an early night, as her exams started in just over one week. She had to cram in as much review as possible, without any distractions. She hit upon an idea, an idea that would suit both of them. After three weeks, her exams would be over, and she'd be free to do whatever she wished. Until then, she suggested that Daniel stay at the resort, where her mother worked. Daniel thought this was strange at first but warmed to the idea of three weeks at a five-star beach resort. She was adamant that this was what she wanted. Daniel agreed, feeling powerless to refuse her wish.

After a beautiful day together, they took a cab back to her campus, where they kissed goodbye. Neither of them wanted to be apart from each other, not even for one night.

When Daniel returned to his hotel room, he made a video call to his mum, eager to share his joy. As soon as Judith saw his smile, she knew her son was happy. He'd already posted a picture of May and himself at the Sky Bar on Facebook. Judith had seen this before he called. She told him how happy he looked and how beautiful May was.

Daniel sensed concern in her voice as she said that she was surprised that so soon after splitting with Emma, he should now have feelings for somebody else. Judith knew firsthand how quickly her son rushed into making decisions without thinking things through first. Even at the age of twenty-five, she worried about his irrational decisions, even more being on his own overseas. He was too trusting and easily led by people.

Judith shed a tear for her son's newfound happiness. "Miss you," she said. "Love you, Danny."

"Miss and love you too, Mum."

At the same resort in Koi Samui, Harrison Fisher was sitting on his bed with his laptop on his knees; he too was video calling his mother. Eva Fisher was busy preparing dinner for her two youngest children in her kitchen at her beach house in Long Island, New York. She placed her laptop on the kitchen counter, away from the prying eyes of her youngest sons, Giles, 6, and Mason, 3. She also turned the volume down, but Harrison was slurring his speech and not making much sense. Eva was fully aware he'd been up all night, drinking and smoking pot; she only just tolerated him in this condition. It was when he was agitated and aggressive that she worried; then she knew he'd been taking cocaine. She herself was now eleven years clean of drugs and knew only too well the effects of cocaine. When she saw Harrison in this condition, she couldn't help but blame herself. She was what she'd call "a terrible mommy."

She was now a changed person, and with this second chance, she was now "a good mommy," who fearlessly protected her two young sons from any form of harm, and when they were older, she would do her utmost to guide them away from any form of narcotic temptation. Eva, unlike her husband, still held onto hope that one day Harrison would be cured of his demons. After endless attempts at rehab and endless counselling sessions forced on him, they now realised he himself had to address his problem and seek help before it was too late.

"You take care, baby," she said.

"I will. Love you, Mom."

CHAPTER 3

Koi Samui

On Friday 13 March, Daniel checked into Dreams Vacation Resort Koi Samui; he stood looking around the ageing reception lounge with disappointment. The main hotel reception was far from impressive; it was only when he saw the superior beach huts that he really appreciated the resort's stunning location and desirability. He was speechless when shown his hut, which stood on stilts not twenty yards from the water's edge. Inside was much roomier than he thought; there was a double bed, desk, plus a futon-style sofa which also became a bed. The decor was simple, rustic, and clean. After unpacking, he sat smoking on his step, staring out to sea, the waters calm, apart from an occasional ripple that formed miniature waves. There was no noise except from the faint sound of music coming from the beach bar in the distance.

The peace and quiet was rudely interrupted by the sound of three rowdy Americans exiting the neighbouring hut, joking and hurling insults at each other. As they were making their way along the beach, the tallest of the three dropped his cigarettes. Daniel ran to pick them up and handed them to him to the tall guy. He thanked him and introduced himself as Harrison Fisher; he also introduced his companions, Ryan and Lucas. After Harrison learned that Daniel was on vacation here alone, he invited him to join them for a beer sometime. Daniel smiled and thanked him, thinking he just might take him up that offer.

In the beach restaurant later that afternoon, Daniel met Phaung for the first time. He found her sitting in the corner of the bar, drinking tea and looking at paperwork through oversized reading glasses. Phaung recognised him instantly and took to her feet to greet him. She asked him to join her for tea. Daniel knew he was about to be interrogated; she was friendly, firm, and very inquisitive. Being his mother's age, he was confused at how old she looked. Behind where he was sitting, he could hear those three American guys he'd seen earlier. Phaung looked over to them with a disconcerting look.

"I'd avoid those boys, Daniel," she said, "especially the tall one. He's a psychopath; he's been causing trouble since he got here two weeks ago."

Daniel turned to see who she was talking about.

"That's Harrison," he said. "I met him earlier; he seemed okay."

Another smartly dressed American tourist, who was sitting at the bar, overheard this and laughed to himself. With a smug grin on his face, he turned to acknowledged he'd overheard their conversation.

Harrison noticed Daniel and called him over to join him for a beer.

"I'd better get back to work," Phaung said. "You join them but be careful." She seemed to struggle getting up from her chair.

Daniel took a chair opposite Harrison, with Ryan and Lucas sitting on either side; they didn't have much interest in this new member of their gang. It was clear Harrison was the leader; he was well spoken, confident, and intelligent. He was good looking with fair hair, cropped into a marine-style haircut. With a Hollywood action hero physique, his looks intimidated Daniel, far more than Jamie ever did. He was a seriously good looking guy. It became clear that Harrison was getting bored with his two young playmate companions, who didn't appear to be his friends of choice; they were nothing more than vacation buddies, thrown together by their wealthy parents.

As Phaung served them beers, a glass accidentally slipped from her hand, spilling onto Ryan's lap. He got mad as hell and jumped up, forcing his chair back and screaming, "Fuck! Look what you've done, lady!"

Lucas laughed, pointing at his groin, and said, "You've pissed your pants, dude!"

Harrison held his hand on his forehead, embarrassed by his friends' behaviour. He shouted, "Enough!"

Phaung ran to fetch a cloth to dry him down, but Harrison stopped her. "No need, ma'am, it's only beer. It'll dry. Would you excuse these juvenile morons for their behaviour?" He took a bundle of Barts from his pocket and held a few of them out to her. "Here, this is for you, ma'am, for all your good service."

Phaung looked at Daniel in disbelief, shocked by his chivalry and generosity; without hesitation, she accepted the money and quickly walked away. Daniel had an inclination that Harrison was trying to impress him, showing off his power and influence. He liked that; his dominance reminded him of Ross. Daniel smiled to himself and wondered what other resemblance he might have to Ross. Perhaps like Ross, underneath that tough-guy exterior was someone who loved being disciplined. Maybe he too liked his American butt spanked?

He was fascinated by Harrison's life; he joked about how he rebelled against his father by getting himself kicked out of Harvard University for supplying cocaine to fellow students. His father was on the list of America's most wealthy, and his mother was once a famous model and actress. Daniel felt like he was being groomed to become Harrison's new playmate and companion; he was flattered that someone of such wealth and stature would find himself of any interest. It was only eight o'clock, but Daniel was tired and had had enough. The more high Harrison became, the more Daniel wanted to leave. He was becoming nauseated.

After he said he needed to leave so he could call May, Ryan and Lucas grew quiet, and Harrison's eyes were filled with anger at the mere suggestion he should leave his company without his authorisation. After a moment, though, Harrison took to his feet and shook his hand, thanking him for his company and wishing him goodnight.

Over breakfast the next morning, Phaung was telling Daniel that Harrison had been ejected from the beach bar last night for being insulting and aggressive to other guests. He was escorted by the same well-dressed guy who was sitting at the bar, the one who overheard their conversation. Daniel knew immediately it was the cocaine, that it wasn't the result of any psychopathic tendencies, as Phaung had thought, although he didn't tell her that. He thought this amusing and wished he'd stayed a little longer to have witnessed him high. As he sat eating breakfast, he watched Ryan and Lucas making their way out of the resort. Lucas called over to him, asking if he wanted to join them on a diving trip. He declined; he wanted to spend some time with his newfound friend, Harrison.

After breakfast, he lay on the beach, sunbathing opposite his own hut, eagerly waiting for Harrison to rise. It was midday before he emerged, wearing boxer shorts and a T-shirt, looking worse for wear after last night. He lit a cigarette and stared out onto the beach from his veranda. Yawning and stretching, he spotted Daniel, who was lying on his front, listening to music through his headphones. Wearing sunglasses and kicking his legs in the air to the beat of his music, Daniel quickly turned away, so as not to appear like he'd being waiting for him.

Harrison signalled for him to come over; he took his glasses off, pretending not to recognise him. Forgetting to put his flip-flops on, his casual walk over quickly turned into a sprint on the scorching hot sand. Harrison couldn't contain his laughter at the sight of him trying to hold in his agony; he invited him to chat whilst he showered and got dressed. Inside, they chatted as Harrison walked into the bathroom whilst he undressed. Daniel couldn't help but check out his body; he gazed lustfully at his pert backside. Suddenly, with embarrassment, Harrison was grinning in the bathroom mirror; he'd seen him checking out his body. From behind, he looked like he had the perfect body, but as he turned to face him, completely naked, he was scarred from his left shoulder down to below his navel. It looked like a large birthmark or scalding wound.

When dressed, he took Daniel to Chi Chi's Beach Bar, next to the resort. He needed to finalise tonight's arrangements for a farewell party he was holding for a girl he'd met. Andrea had been his friend and confidant since arriving here two weeks ago. At the bar, Harrison disappeared with a staff member, leaving Daniel standing alone, next to the smartly dressed American guy from yesterday. His attempts of a friendly conversation proved to be a struggle, although he did manage to get his name. Parker was an ex-cop from Florida who was now working in New York City. When he asked why he was here in Koi Samui, he made it clear he had no intention of continuing the conversation.

Daniel was shocked by his rudeness; he ordered a pitcher of beer and took a table to wait for Harrison. As he kicked off his sandals and relaxed, he admired the beautiful people on the stunning beach. He felt a hand on his shoulder; it was Harrison, clutching two whisky chasers.

"Don't worry about him, he's an asshole," he said, referring to Parker.

The whisky chasers were to sort his head out after last night. Daniel wasn't sure if he was on a cocaine downer or he was actually depressed. He talked about how lonely he was; even with having a girlfriend, friends, and family back in New York, he still felt lonely and ostracised. The only person close to him was a guy called Carlos, but he was selective on the details of how he knew him. Daniel thought perhaps he was his secret gay lover.

Harrison was slowly becoming intrigued by his new English playmate. Unlike his other companions, he was genuine and down to earth. His British humour made him laugh, something which rarely happened. He had no interest in discussing May. Daniel sensed this and never mentioned her again. He knew he liked him; like with Auguste, he was on a confidence high, flattered that somebody of his stature could find him attractive. But unlike Auguste, he felt like a servant, whose aim was to please his master, a feeling that scared him but excited him even more.

Andrea spotted them chatting from the beach; she and three of her friends invited themselves to join them. Harrison moved around the table to make room, sitting closely to Daniel. They turned to each other, annoyed their time together had been rudely interrupted. Just looking into his eyes, it became obvious that Harrison was seeking more than just a playmate. As a surprise to Daniel himself, he felt the same. This also became apparent to Andrea; she stared at Daniel, grinning, as if she knew what was running through his mind.

As the girls looked through the menu, Harrison showed Daniel where the washroom was. Inside, he went straight into a cubicle, dragging Daniel in with him. He took out his wallet; inside was a small bag of cocaine. He cut two lines up on the cistern, snorted the first line, and then handed the straw to Daniel. The euphoria hit him almost immediately; his desire for Harrison intensified almost beyond his control. Harrison dipped his finger into the last remaining white powder and rubbed it onto his gums. Daniel grabbed his hand, guiding his finger into his own mouth, and then licked the tip of his finger with his lips clenched. He guided his finger slowly in and out of his mouth, his heart beat racing to a level that scared him. He panicked and bolted for the door. Harrison begged him not to leave; he raced over to the sink to splash cold water on his face. As he stared at himself in the mirror, he could just about see a reflection on the cubicle floor of Harrison masturbating.

He stumbled back to the table, trying compose himself. It was now full of appetisers and bottles of wine; he poured himself a glass to calm his nerves, unaware that the biggest shock was yet to come. Harrison returned from the washroom, smiling; he looked happy, a contrast to his earlier mood.

He looked at the table full of food and said, "Mmmmm, Thai finger buffet. Daniel, your favourite!"

Daniel, embarrassed by this, nearly spat out his wine. As Andrea and her friends chatted away about tonight's beach party, Harrison, who handed Daniel a platter of mini shrimp wraps. His left hand discreetly disappeared under the table. Daniel felt that hand touch his leg; his leg muscles tightened with fear as Harrison's hand gently stoked his inner thigh. His hand explored into his shorts, brushing his testicles with his little finger.

Daniel coughed with shock. Andrea passed him a bottle of water. She knew where Harrison hand was; she smiled at him, just to make him feel that little bit more uncomfortable. She found this amusing. Harrison's hand went deeper into his shorts to find his now erect penis; he gripped it tightly and then massaged it, causing Daniel to moan silently to himself. His heart began to race and his breathing changed; his knees began to tremble before a surge of sexual ecstasy sent him into orgasm, forcing him to climax into Harrison's hand. Harrison turned to him with a slight grin, asking him if he was okay. The conversation at the table fell silent as everybody turned to stare at Daniel, concerned about his odd behaviour.

Daniel made an excuse that he'd drank too much wine in the sun and needed to lie down. He left the table, flushed and embarrassed, trying to compose himself; worst still was when Harrison stood up, wiping his hand with a napkin, and invited him to a party there that evening. Daniel said his goodbyes and staggered back to his hut, biting his bottom lip, grinning, happy, and high. This was the risky fun he'd always craved, yet all he wanted now was to collapse in a darkened room with the air con on full.

Surprisingly, he managed to sleep that afternoon, after a thousand thoughts raced through his mind. He felt no guilt for his behaviour today; this didn't change his feeling towards May. He convinced himself that the situation with Harrison was nothing more than harmless fun.

He woke at 8.30 p.m., feeling refreshed and excited, looking forward to tonight's beach party. He showered, singing along to his favourite tunes of Paolo Natini and Ed Sheeran. Before getting dressed, he admired his newly slimmed-down figure. His weight was now falling off; this and the attention of Auguste, May, and Harrison put his confidence at an all-time high. As he walked along the beach, he could hear the chilled-out dance music being played at Chi Chi's. As he got closer, he could smell Thai food being cooked. The beach was alight with bamboo lanterns and campfires, the sand covered by colourful rustic rugs and oversized cushions. People lay around, chatting, surrounded by ice buckets filled with bottles.

The party was an extravagant farewell gesture for Andrea and her friends, who were leaving tomorrow. All twelve of them were invited, plus their newfound friends and holiday fuck buddies, organised and paid for by Harrison. There was no expense spared; he was very generous with his father's money. Harrison was the first person Daniel recognised; he stood out from the crowd. He reminded him of a Hollywood heart-throb taking a timeout, chilling and relaxing from shooting a blockbuster movie. He was lying next to Andrea, both facing different directions. Not far away from them was Ryan and Lucas, who were also lying next to their new female companions.

Daniel felt this party was being held in his honour by the way Harrison greeted him. He was overjoyed to see him and sat him in between himself and Andrea, who only turned briefly to acknowledge he'd arrived. She was planning something of a secret with one of her friends. Daniel quickly downed two beers, feeling he needed to catch up with everybody. However, no amount of beers could put him the state as the other guests; looking around, he could easily identify what drugs each person was taking. It wasn't long before Harrison whisked him away to the washroom to get him high. When they returned to beach, Andrea's secret plan was revealed. She wanted all the men to strip naked and stand shoulder to shoulder, covering their genitalia, with the sea behind them; she wanted to photograph them. She and her mates wanted this photo for their social media page. She didn't need to ask twice; they all started stripping, but Daniel was hesitant. It wasn't his penis he was scared of showing to the public, it was his body.

23

Harrison was one of the first to get naked, with one hand over his penis, he stood over him, trying to convince him to strip. He then ordered Lucas and Ryan to hold his arms down whilst he undressed him.

Daniel wriggled at first until Harrison started to unbutton his shirt; the sensation of being held down whilst being undressed started to arouse him. When Harrison reached his shorts, Daniel begged him to stop, for fear of serious embarrassment. This didn't stop him; in fact, it provoked him further. He reached slowly to pull his shorts down whilst his palm rubbed up against his visible erection. Sure enough, as he pulled his shorts down, out popped his stiff penis. Harrison looked at it with lust and smiled; he winked at him whilst staring lovingly into his eyes. However, not letting the opportunity go to waste, he then shouted at the top of his voice, "Everybody, we've got timber over here!"

By this time, Daniel couldn't care less; he took to his feet and stood in line for the photo shoot. After the session was finished and they headed back to their clothes, two girls were laughing and pointing in Daniel's direction; one said, "Hey, there's the fat guy with the stiffy."

Harrison overheard this and jumped to his defence, loudly. He pointed at them and shouted, "Hey ladies, it's your turn to get naked. Yeah, you. What's wrong, honey? You shy about getting your tiny titties out? Hey sweetie, yeah you, you over there with the butt the size of a beach hut! There's plenty of guys here desperate to see that big fat ass."

Their laughter soon stopped, and then suddenly, the boyfriend of beach-hut butt lady ran over to him to shut him up, followed by Parker, who was drinking in the bar. As the boyfriend began to throw a punch at him, Harrison grabbed his wrist and twisted it behind his back. As Parker approached them to break it up, Harrison pushed the boyfriend's face down into the sand. Parker then grabbed hold of the boyfriend to stop him following Harrison. Nobody said a word; they just watched, stunned, scared to speak.

Daniel was watching this, sitting next to Andrea. She turned to him and murmured, "Somebody's trying to impress someone?"

It was 2.30 a.m. Chinese lanterns were sent sailing off into the moonlit sky. Andrea thanked Harrison for the eventful party, and then she and her crew called it a night. By four o'clock, the remaining guests, who were either drunk or stoned, lay semi-unconscious around their campfires, which were now nothing more than glowing embers. Lucas and Ryan had both disappeared with their ladies. This wasn't by choice; Harrison insisted they leave just him and Daniel alone together.

After they left, now both stoned, they lay on their backs and stared up at the stars. Without saying a word, they turned to each other and smiled, both happy in each other's company. From the distance, Daniel spotted Parker sitting at the bar. The bar was now closed, and it was dark; he could just see the outline of him, smoking and staring at them. Curious, he walked over to him. As he got closer, Parker told him to take a seat opposite him. With his arms crossed, he leant forward speak.

"He's making a fool of you," he said seriously. "You're nothing more than a novelty to him. A rough northern English novelty. Look around this island, Daniel, look at the other good-looking guys he could get to fulfil his homosexual appetite! That old lady at the restaurant; I hear you've got the hots for her daughter. Pretty girl, I believe, and intelligent; what would she make of you throwing yourself at a man?"

Daniel stood up; he'd heard enough. Still stoned, his mind addled, he could hardly grasp or comprehend what he was saying.

Before he turned to walk back to Harrison, Parker angrily told him, "You take my advice; stay away from him, you hear me?"

At breakfast the next morning, Phaung was nowhere to be seen. Daniel asked the other staff members where she was; she'd apparently fainted at work yesterday. They suspected exhaustion; she been advised to take two days bed rest. Lucas, Ryan, and their female friends were on their way out of the resort for yet another boring boat trip. On this occasion, due to wanting to impress their female companions, he didn't invite him.

Completely disregarding Parker's advice, Daniel quickly made his way to Harrison's hut. When he arrived at the door, he overheard him having a phone conversation with somebody. Before knocking, he held back for a while; the conversation was about himself.

He overheard Harrison saying, "He's cute, he makes me laugh, he's unlike anybody I've met before."

As he listened closely, from out of nowhere, Parker appeared. Not wanting any confrontation with him, Daniel quickly knocked at the door. Harrison answered immediately, with his phone still against his ear. He spotted Parker leering in their direction and quickly hung up.

Before Daniel had chance to speak, Harrison grabbed his bag and said, "You coming for a boat trip, Daniel. Let's get the fuck out of here!"

As they walked off together to join Lucas and Ryan, Daniel turned back to see Parker, who was smiling and shaking his head. The boat trip was merely an excuse to consume as much alcohol as physically possible, with a little help from the white powder in Harrison's bag. The day was a riotous party. They were both inseparable; they talked and joked, as intimate as the other seagoers would allow. They promised each other that the next day would be just the two of them alone.

The next day, they secretly stocked up with beers and snuck away to spend the day together in Daniel's hut, just the two of them, hiding away from the outside world. It was Harrison who set the pace; it was common for him to take charge and to be in control. He lay on the bed and told Daniel about his upbringing. Daniel listened intently.

"My mom had me when she was just twenty. She'd only been married for a year. I wasn't planned; I was an accident, an unwanted accident. Her career was just taking off; the last thing she wanted was a baby. She had a coke habit back in those days; when she learned she was pregnant, she thought it would damage her career if people knew she'd aborted a baby at such a late stage. While she was travelling the world modelling and Dad was busy building up his empire, they entrusted our housekeeper, Maria, to become my nanny.

"At first she was nice; she brought me up, loving me as she would her own. Weirdly, though, she began to believe I was her own child. As the years went by, she became twisted and bitter. She resented my parents' wealth and turned against me. It got to a stage that she couldn't even look at me. I sensed her resentment and hatred towards me; as much as I tried to shy away from her, it just made her worse. Morning after morning, I'd wake up in a wet bed, thinking I'd wet myself, until one night, I woke to find her pouring her own pee onto my bed; she did this to make out I was a difficult child, so she could hold out for more money.

"She was a true sadist; she took great pleasure in seeing me in pain. One morning, I sat at the table, waiting for my boiled eggs. She spooned the eggs into cups and calmly placed them on the table, and then she casually lifted the pan of boiling water and poured it over my shoulder. You know what, Daniel? She just turned the volume up on the TV to drown out the sound of me screaming in agony. She made out to my parents that it was me who pulled the pan from the cooker; of course, she was very convincing. One day, I overheard her talking with a reporter; she was trying to sell a story about my mother's coke habit. I told my dad; he was furious. Only then did he listen to me! Not when I was being tortured by her, oh no. But when his precious family's reputation was in danger, only then did he wise up on her.

"He wired our house in Long Island with spy cameras; they got their proof, all right. Back then, I was told she was taken back to Texas, where she came from, but that's another story. Of course, no cops were involved; my dad didn't want the media involved. You see, Daniel, I had one fucked-up childhood."

Daniel was moved by this; it completely changed his opinion of Harrison as a spoilt rich kid who'd had it easy. He leant forward and held him; as their eyes met, a kiss was inevitable. At first, Daniel hesitated; even though he'd done almost everything sexual with Ross, he'd never kissed a man before. The kiss was electric, pleasurable, like nothing he'd ever experienced.

After they kiss, Harrison reached for his small bag of cocaine and shook it in front of Daniel's face.

"Let's get wasted," he said, smiling.

They both sat on the floor and snorted lines off Harrison's laptop, and then he showed Daniel photographs of his life back in the United States. He was astonished by how wealthy Harrison's family was. He showed photographs of his family, including his mother, who he remembered seeing on a 1990s US sitcom. She was stunningly beautiful, even now in her late forties. He also recognised his father, from newspaper articles on the richest Americans. He was amazed by their properties: a skiing chalet in Tremblant, Canada, used for holidays; a mansion in Manhattan, which was Billy's weekday residence, and where Eva occasionally stayed when she shopped and socialised in the city; an apartment in Brooklyn, where Harrison lived; a beach house in North Fork, Long Island, where Eva stayed when Billy was in the city; and a mansion in Westhampton, where the family all came together at weekends. He also showed him photographs of his prized possession: his beloved personalised, super-charged, blacked-out Range Rover Sport, which was bought for him as a twenty-first birthday present. Daniel was impressed; he wanted a similar car.

As the hours passed by, Harrison's little bag of coke began to run low. He reached for his phone to call a courier to deliver more to the hotel. He asked Daniel if he'd collect it from Dougie at the main entrance, outside reception.

"Can't you pick it up yourself?" he asked suspiciously.

"People are watching me," Harrison said. "I'm being followed!"

He was high at this point; Daniel thought he was having a drug-induced paranoid episode.

"It's simple and safe; no risk, trust me! Dougie works as a vacation representative. He'll shake your hand and pass you an envelope; inside, there is nothing more than excursion leaflets. The coke will be passed to you in his other hand. No money exchanged; it's on account. Perfectly safe; please, do it for me, Daniel."

He felt honoured to be running such an errand for him, and as usual, the element of danger got the better of him; he agreed.

Just thirty minutes later, Daniel stood nervously smoking outside the main entrance, unsure of what he'd let himself in for. Sure enough, as planned, Dougie pulled up next to him, driving an inconspicuous Toyota Yaris. He was smartly dressed, wearing a short-sleeved blue shirt, colourful striped tie, and black trousers; he was even wearing a name tag on his shirt pocket, looking like your average tour-rep. He quickly jumped out to shake Daniel's hand and passed him the envelope; the deal was done. As Dougie jumped back into his car, Daniel turned to head back into the reception; as the sliding doors opened, to Daniel's horror, Parker came out, talking on his mobile phone, shaking his head and looking towards his direction. Terrified by this, Daniel's legs went to jelly, and his heartbeat began to race. There was something suspicious about this man that put the fear of God into him. The fact that he was an ex-cop didn't help.

Daniel calmly walked back into reception; there was no doubt in his mind Parker knew what he'd just collected. Before he reached the door that led out onto the beach, he turned to see if he was still watching. Sure enough, as he'd dreaded, he'd finished his phone call and was staring at him. He held his hand to his head to mimic a gun and then mouthed word "Bang." Daniel, now terrified, turned and quickly made his way back to his hut.

The relief of being safely back in his hut was overwhelming; his hand was still trembling with fear as he locked the door behind him. Harrison had been eagerly awaiting his return; he gave him a sympathetic hug for his ordeal and wasted no time chopping up two lines. Now safely locked away, it was time for them to get high again, only this time they wanted to jointly enter a world with no morals and no inhibitions. Both high, they sat facing each other on the bed, happily agreeing that they'd never leave each other's side again There was no place they'd rather be than being together, high on cocaine. The outside world could go fuck itself now that they were inseparable. That was, until May called Daniel on his mobile.

He knew it was her calling him and quickly tried to reach for his phone without Harrison seeing her name flash up on the screen. It was too late; Harrison got there first. He held the phone in his hands, looking furiously at her name.

"What the fuck does she want?" he spat. "I'm warning you, Daniel, you're not speaking to her. I'll answer it and tell the bitch to fuck off!"

Daniel quickly reached over and managed to grab the phone from his hand. As he ran to the door, Harrison jumped up from the bed to chase him. Before he could escape through the door, Harrison grabbed his arm tightly from behind and bashed it against the wall. The phone dropped from his hand. The force of his arm hitting the wall smashed his watch; it shattered into tiny pieces and trickled on to the floor.

Daniel stared in disbelief at floor, dreading what was coming next. Harrison grabbed his shoulder turning him around, "Look at me, Daniel. I said look at me!" Daniel looked up and stared fearfully into his eyes. "I poured my heart out to you today. I told you things I've never spoken about to anybody. This was supposed to be our day, our time alone together, with no interruptions, not from anybody."

Daniel shook his head defiantly and walked away, saying, "We're nothing more than friends, fooling around and getting high together. It's no big deal. Besides, I wanted to talk to her. I miss her; to be honest, you were becoming nauseating, needy, and dull."

Daniel's heart was racing with fear as he waited for his reaction. Harrison smiled and tilted his head slightly to one side whilst staring deep into his eyes, analysing and digesting what he'd just said. He knew he was lying, just saying it to hurt him; he thought for a moment how to respond. Suddenly, with both hands, he overpowered him, pressing him up against the wall. He started to kiss him passionately.

Daniel didn't struggle; he had a plan. He pretended to enjoy the kiss until he released his grip. When that happened, he seized the opportunity and started to lift up Harrison's vest. As he raised it above his head, with his arms in the air, he pushed him backwards with all his strength. He tripped, and his towering body fell crashing backwards onto the wooden floor with an almighty thud. His head hit the desk on the way down. As he lay there, he didn't move or make a sound. He remained silent, his eyes open, staring motionless at the ceiling.

Daniel panicked; he slowly walked over to the lifeless body, fearing he'd killed him. In horror, with his hands over his mouth, he could see blood slowly trickling along a groove in the wood flooring, seeping from the back of Harrison's head. With his hands pressed against his mouth, he knelt down to look at him closely.

"Oh fuck, oh fuck, what have I done? Wake up, please, please, wake up, I'm sorry!"

Tears began to fall from his eyes, but then suddenly, Harrison grinned and burst into laughter. He then reached his hand around to the back of his head to examine his wound.

"It's just a cut, you dumb-ass; you're such a pussy. Jeeze, you English guys, you sure do like to play rough," he said whilst looking at his blood-soaked fingers. "Did you think I was dead? Were you upset, were you saddened my violent demise? You ain't getting rid of me that easy, that's for sure!"

As much as Daniel was relieved he was okay, he'd had just about enough for one day. He got up and opened the door, begging Harrison to leave. He left without saying a word; he just stared at him with a sad, puppy-dog expression. Daniel slammed the door behind him; he looked around the hut, only to find he'd forgotten his laptop.

Shit, he said to himself as he dropped to the floor, holding his head in his hands. His head was in turmoil.

He didn't leave the hut for the rest of the night; he only opened the door once to take two bottles of red wine he asked to be sent down from the restaurant. He only drank red wine when he was coming down from a high; it helped him to relax and sleep. He called May to apologise for not answering her call and his mum to let her know how much he was enjoying Koi Samui. Before he got into bed, he noticed Harrison's black vest, hanging from the side of a litter bin. Earlier, after he'd cleaned the blood stain from the floor, he'd spotted it and wanted to be rid of every single trace of him. Back then, he was still angry with him, but now, after drinking the wine, the lust he had for him returned.

He reached for the vest and held it against his face. He could smell his aftershave; he could almost feel him standing next to him. He became aroused; he undressed and lay naked on the bed, masturbating. He fantasised that Harrison suddenly walked in on him masturbating on his bed. He'd called to collect his belongings and wanted to say farewell. Before parting for good, he lay next to him on the bed; there was no intercourse, just gently touching and examining each other's bodies.

He'd never fantasised about sex with another man before; it was always women. This terrified him. Especially when the man he was having fantasies about was the same person he hated so much that he wanted cause him physical harm. Throughout his sleepless night, he thought about May. He imagined how good they looked together and how people, especially Emma and Jamie, who would be sickeningly jealous that he should have such a beautiful girlfriend.

He slept in till eleven the next morning and went to the beach restaurant for a late breakfast. Phaung was back at work. Harrison and his crew were nowhere to be seen. Phaung told him that they took a flight to Bangkok; Harrison had asked if she could recommend a hotel there. Phaung was under the impression he was fishing to find out where May worked. She didn't tell him, wary of Daniel; she was unsure about his motives. Daniel was relieved; he looked at her inquisitively, wondering why she was reluctant to tell him.

"My daughter only has eyes for you," she said, reassuring him.

This didn't change the fear he had for why he'd wanted to see her. Phaung knew most things about the guests staying at resort; this came with being brought into conversations, usually from backpackers passing through who would get bored of talking about places they'd visited and turn their attentions to gossiping about people's lives.

It was four days since he'd last seen Harrison and his crew. He knew they were not due to leave until Sunday morning, and their belongings were still in their hut. Daniel had spent the past four days sunbathing, swimming, and working out in the resort's gym. He felt fit, healthy, and relaxed; things were looking good. Even though he spoke to May several times a day, there was somebody he missed dreadfully; that person was Harrison. On Saturday, the day before they were due to fly back to New York, Daniel spent most of the day waiting patiently near his hut, knowing Harrison would have to call to collect his laptop.

It was afternoon when he finally showed up at the resort. Daniel thought it best not to ask him why he'd tried to find out where May worked. With him leaving the next morning, he didn't want him going with any animosity between them. On this occasion, Harrison was thoughtful, kind, and sensitive. He behaved like a true gentleman; it suited him. Miraculously, he'd managed to stay away from drugs whilst in Bangkok. Also, whilst there, he'd bought him a gift: a replacement watch.

Daniel was overjoyed, not by the watch, but how his face beamed with joy as he handed him the surprise gift. Like himself, he noticed he took great pleasure in giving; he liked this in a person. Apart from calling to collect his laptop and give him the gift, he'd also dropped by to invite him to Chi Chi's for farewell drinks. Daniel, still slightly wary of him, hesitated slightly; knowing there would be alcohol and maybe drugs involved, he was unsure whether to accept his invitation.

"Hey, don't let me down. Be nice for you and I to say goodbye properly," Harrison said sincerely.

For fuck sake, he said to himself, *just go. What harm could a few farewell drinks do?* He smiled and accepted.

Before leaving for Chi Chi's that night, he chatted to May whilst he surfed the net, trying to value the watch. He felt a sense of relief that Harrison was leaving tomorrow, a relief that he could now give his full attention to her, without any distractions. He knew he was attracted to him, but he thought maybe he was nothing more than distraction whilst he waited for May. He'd never been comfortable, alone by himself; he'd always had close companions by his side.

Maybe Harrison was a replacement for his best friend Jamie, he thought, trying to convince himself. As they chatted on his mobile, he suddenly cried, "Fuck me!" Then he went quiet; speechless, he stared at the screen, his eyes and mouth wide open in disbelief.

"Danny, Danny are you there?" May asked.

"Yes, yes, I'm here. Sorry, I was distracted. May, I need to go. I'll call tomorrow."

He quickly hung up; he was staring at the same Tag Heuer watch, for sale in a department store in Bangkok. Its price was a staggering £29,000.

"This is ridiculous, why would anybody spend this amount of money on somebody they just met?" he asked himself as he gently caressed the watch with his fingers.

At Chi Chi's, the mood was sombre. He sat sandwiched in between Ryan and Lucas, who endlessly moaned about how rough they were feeling after three weeks in Koi Samui. Both were looking forward to returning to their privileged lifestyles back in Long Island. Three weeks of heavy drinking, drug taking, and shagging had taken its toll on them. Harrison was sitting opposite; with one hand, he twirled a lighter through his fingers, and with the other, he was flicking peanuts from the table, trying to aim them into a litter bin. He looked bored, frustrated, and angry; he only spoke when it was time to order more drinks.

After an hour of listening to endless moaning from his immature friends, he angrily stood up and insisted Daniel accompany him to the washroom. Daniel knew what awaited him in there; now bored himself, he was relieved by the invite. Harrison raced ahead, and by the time he entered the washroom, he already had a straw up his nose, crouching over the toilet cistern.

"My whole existence has been a disaster. I'm so fucked up," Harrison said as he stood up to allow Daniel to take his turn. "Hey, you could come with me. You can come back with me to New York, or I could stay here with you; we could go anywhere together, just you and me. There's nothing or nobody for me to go back for. Well, there is someone, but it's complicated. I'll tell you about him some other time. I'm not sure of many things, but I'm sure about you. I can give you a good life, and you can make my life worth living!"

Daniel stood up and wiped his nose; he turned to him with an immediate high and laughed. "You crack me up; seriously, you make me laugh!"

Harrison looked at him with anger in his eyes but then smiled; he turned and casually washed his hands in the sink whilst looking at his reflection in the mirror. He turned again and furiously punched a paper towel dispenser whilst heading for the door. Daniel's laughter stopped. Suddenly, realising he was serious, he tried to call him back whilst trying to compose himself.

Parker was sitting at the bar when he got outside; he was just about to turn in for the night. Harrison told him he was too, and they both walked in opposite directions back to their huts. When out sight of each other, Harrison turned back and ordered a bottle of wine from the bar, as Daniel stumbled back to the table.

"Here, I bought you this," Harrison said as he poured him a large glass.

As Daniel drank his wine, Harrison became agitated and nervous; after just one glass, he thanked him but insisted he'd take the rest back to his hut to drink. He suddenly felt unwell. After just one glass, he felt like he had drank three bottles. His speech was slurred, and his vision became impaired. Unsteadily, he took to his feet to say his goodbyes. Ryan offered to walk him back to his hut, but Harrison insisted he should be the one to escort him.

They didn't talk on the way back to his hut; the bottle fell from Daniel's hand as he tried to focus on walking in a straight line. At the door, he struggled with his keys. Harrison took them from his hand to open up. After he walked into the darkened hut, Harrison locked the door behind them and started to undressed Daniel. Now face down on his bed, he was still conscious but struggling to move.

"Have you drugged me?" he asked. "Am I going to die?" He managed to turn his head, seeking a response.

"After I've fucked you, yes, you'll probably die ... I'll make sure our last night together is special!"

Daniel could just make out the silhouette of Harrison's naked body standing next to his bed; he was staring down at him whilst ripping a condom wrapper open with his teeth. Harrison had tears in his eyes as he climbed on top of him and forced his penis into his anus.

"We could have been good together. I'll leave you with this reminder of me, one you'll never forget!"

CHAPTER 4

Time for Healing

On this morning, the sun didn't shine. It was overcast, almost dark; nobody was on the beach. Every morning since he'd arrived, he could overhear conversations from sunbathers and the occasional children's laughter. But this morning, all he could hear was the sound of somebody knocking at the door. His eyes stayed closed; that's the way he wanted it. Well, just for now. He only moved his head to avoid the vile stench of his vomit next to where his mouth lay open on the pillow. The knocking at the door stopped; his body was not quite ready to move yet, for fear of pain. He remembered this pain well from his first attempt at anal sex with Ross. He remembered screaming the place down in agony and then laughing about it. Unlike Harrison, Ross withdrew himself at the slightest suggestion of causing him any pain; looking back, Ross was a good guy. As he lay there, he remembered everything about last night, even to the tiniest of detail of that moment he thought he was about to die. He even remembered Harrison's moaning with pleasure just as he was about to orgasm and how, as he left, he didn't check to see if he was still breathing after viciously violating his body.

He could hear a key inside the lock. The door opened; it was Parker. He'd spoken to Phaung, who'd managed to get him a spare key. He told her not to enter and closed the door so she couldn't see. At first, he was speechless at the sight of his lifeless body lying naked with vomit on his pillow and traces of blood from his anal passage. He crept towards him, believing he was dead, but then he jumped with fear as Daniel spoke.

"What are you doing here, Parker? Is this what you'd warned me about? You can leave now safe in the knowledge you were right, and I was wrong."

"I'll be here if you need me, Daniel. When you're ready to talk, I'll be here," Parker said and left him alone.

Phaung was still waiting for him outside. Daniel overheard him tell her he'd been sick and wasn't up to any visitors. All that was left for him was to get out of bed, clean up, and try to embrace the day. Still lying in the same position, he cried like he'd never cried before.

He emerged from his hut at lunch in search of alcohol. Phaung shouted to say hello as he made his way to a nearby supermarket; he didn't acknowledge her. On the way back, he held his head down, in fear of any conversation with her. He just wanted to shut himself away and submerge himself in a bottle of vodka.

That same morning, at Daniel's home in Middleton, Manchester, Judith had a visitor; it was Emma. She'd brought over a photo of the ultrasound of the baby. Judith was delighted, even more when she told her she was having a boy. Judith made it clear after Daniel left that she was still the baby's grandmother; even though Emma was now with Jamie, she promised to always be there for her. On Emma's return home, Jamie told her Daniel had made four attempts to video call her. She was worried that there was a problem, and she also wanted to show him the photograph, so she tried to call him. When Daniel answered, she was devastated by his condition.

He answered the video call squatting on floor, incoherent and distressed. He struggled to form a sentence. Blood was dripping from the side of his face, seeping from a cut eyebrow. His eyes looked tired, unable to focus, and he looked like he'd lost a lot of weight. He didn't make much sense, and he blamed Emma for what had happened and why he was in this state. When Emma asked what had happened, he shook his head as if it was too painful to talk about it. Daniel fell backward and went into a seizure; Emma was in tears, watching as Jamie comforted her; he himself was alarmed at what unfolded before his eyes. They heard knocking at his door; a woman walked in, holding her hand to her mouth with fear at the sight of Daniel having a fit. She was with a security guard, who quickly called for medical help. Emma canceled the call; she was too distraught to watch any more.

Daniel woke the next morning in a private room at the Samui International Hospital, in surprisingly high spirits. All he remembered about yesterday was that he had been on a mission of self-destruction. Before the doctor saw him, he rang Emma for fear of her telling Judith. He told her his drink had been spiked; she didn't believe him but was glad he was fine now. She hadn't told Judith for fear of upsetting her. He also called Phaung; she had found him and called for help. He pleaded with her not to tell May; she agreed and asked him to see her when he returned to the resort.

The doctor alerted Daniel to the high levels of Xanax in his blood; Xanax was commonly used as a date rape drug here in Thailand. The combination of Xanax and alcohol was to blame for his seizure; if he hadn't have been found, or if he'd drank more alcohol, this could have proved fatal. He was lucky to be alive; he was allowed back to the resort on the condition he drank plenty of fluids and rested. Whilst he was there, he asked to doctor for advice on bleeding from his anus; after an examination, he was told there was nothing to worry about, nothing more than a tear in the rectum tissue. The doctor asked if there was anything else he'd like talk about; by his sympathetic expression, he obviously he knew what had happened.

"Not now, but thank you," Daniel replied.

"Mr Reed, the records of your treatment and your examination have been recorded, should you need to access them in the future."

After his return to the resort, he couldn't face the hut; he asked to be moved. The only accommodation available at that time was a three-bedroom premier bungalow, commonly reserved for wealthy families. Without hesitation, Daniel booked it, asking that it be ready as soon as possible. Before returning to the hut, he went to see Phaung. She was happy to see him; his condition yesterday upset her, far more than she'd admitted. Yesterday, before his video call to Emma, Phaung found him lying face down on the pathway that ran parallel to the beach; he was en route to the supermarket to buy more alcohol. She escorted him back to his hut, insisting he not drink any more. Thirty minutes later, she returned with a resort security guard to check on him. That was when they found him in seizure. Daniel broke into tears when he heard this; he apologised from his heart for upsetting her and thanked her for calling for help.

He was now about to face the moment he'd dreaded: returning to the hut. The hut looked like it had been thoroughly cleaned. It was spotless; even his clothes had been washed, pressed, and folded. As he started to pack, Parker knocked at the open door. He was smiling; he told Daniel he had organised this special cleaning service.

"I don't understand," Daniel said. "Why you did that?"

"I thought I was doing you a favour."

"Yes, thank you, but I need to ask you something. I need to report what happened to the police; Parker, will you be a witness? The hospital found Xanax in my blood. Harrison had spiked my drink."

"Yes, yes, of course I will, but Daniel, you were both using drugs. You supplied Harrison with cocaine; I saw you, remember? I know about these things, I'm an ex-cop. I wouldn't involve the police, not here in Thailand, and especially where drugs are involved."

"Then I'll report it to the American police," Daniel said. "I have to do something."

"His father's a wealthy man; he'll have the best lawyers in the country. I'm sorry to tell you this, but there's not much you can do about it. I'll leave you now. I'm off to New Zealand tomorrow for a new job. I'll bid you farewell. Best of luck, man."

After he left, it took him ten minutes to pack; he couldn't wait to get the hell out of there. The bungalow was stunning, extremely private, set a little back from the beach, with a large veranda looking out to sea. It was specious inside, with plenty of rooms for him to wander around.

The next few days went by; he worked out in the gym twice a day, determined to change his body and mind and soul. He even had his long floppy hair trimmed to a short spiked cut. He wanted to be reborn; the old Daniel had died in the hut that night.

He and Phaung became good friends; she even spoke to his mother via video call. Judith was slightly envious of this woman, who had become her overseas replacement, but in reality, she was delighted he had found somebody older and wiser to look out for him, someone he could call a friend.

May was due to land in Koi Samui in just three days' time; he felt optimistic his relationship with her would flourish and Harrison would be pushed to the back of his mind, dead and buried in the past, and so he was, until a drunken night at Chi Chi's.

Daniel had spotted a Norwegian guy who resembled Harrison; his looks were uncanny, apart from his heavily tattooed arms. The more alcohol he drank, the more he resembled him; he couldn't take his eyes off him. The Norwegian guy grew aware he was being leered at and became irritated and uncomfortable, fuelling Daniel to leer even more. When he went to the washroom, Daniel seized the opportunity and followed him, unsure as to what his own intentions were. As he stood next to him at the urinals, he felt a surge of fear and anticipation to what was about to happen, and then he asked, "You look like a fag; do you give good head?"

The guy finished urinating and calmly put his penis away; he fastened his shorts and then threw a fist at Daniel's face. He struck him in the mouth and then panicked and rushed out of the bathroom. Daniel turned to see his reflection in the mirror; he smiled at the sense of being in control of his own pain and discomfort. As his lip started to bleed and swell, he felt relief; this was his decision, and he had an overwhelming feeling of being in control.

On the beach the next morning, Daniel was happily sunbathing, humming away to his favourite tunes through his earphones. He opened his eyes to a shadow blocking out his sun; surprisingly, it was the Norwegian guy from last night. He quickly took off his headphones, unsure as to what to expect.

"I came to apologise," the man said. "I'm not in the habit of hitting anyone, especially someone who's had too much alcohol to drink."

"No, no apology needed," Daniel replied. "I provoked you. I'm the one who's sorry."

He introduced himself, and they shook hands; his name was Bardo, and he was from Stavanger, Norway. He was staying here with four of his friends; they'd only arrived here yesterday. Daniel felt ridiculous; in the light of day, he looked nothing like Harrison. He felt guilty knowing he'd provoked him on his first night here; just as he turned to leave, he stopped for a moment.

"Can I ask you one question, Daniel? How did you know I was gay?"

"I didn't," Daniel said. "I thought you were straight; you reminded me of somebody, so I wanted you to hit me. Please don't ask me why."

"Okay, I need to go now. I'm meeting my friends. Maybe later today, we could have a drink together."

"I'd like that. I'd like that a lot,"

Daniel invited him to join him for wine later; he pointed to his bright blue bungalow, where he spent the afternoons sitting in the shade on the veranda. Later that afternoon, Bardo arrived to a warm welcome. Daniel had ordered nibbles; fresh fruit and white wine were all laid out on the veranda's dining table. He felt as comfortable talking to Bardo as he did with Auguste; no pressure, just new friends getting to know each other.

"So this person I remind you of, did he break your heart?"

"You could say that."

At first, Daniel wasn't sure whether to tell him the truth. It was a pleasant evening, both enjoying each other's company, drinking chilled wine and looking out to sea at the sunset. He felt he'd be darkening the mood.

"I'd like to know, seriously, what did this person do to make you want to antagonise me into hitting you?"

Daniel told him what happened that night; Bardo was appalled and disgusted.

"When I saw you last night, I felt disgusted with myself for being attracted to you. I felt I needed to be punished. Don't get me wrong, I detest what he's done to me. He's violated my body and twisted my mind with his toxin."

"Were you in love with him?"

"I'm unsure; whatever I felt for him is history. I'm burning with anger and thoughts of revenge. I want to destroy him and make him suffer. Then when I've succeeded, perhaps I can stop hating myself."

"Have you thought how you will do this?"

"I have no idea, as yet. I've been advised not to report it here in Thailand; there were drugs involved."

"Where are you travelling to after this vacation?"

"I'm not sure yet. I met a girl here in Thailand; my dream is to do an American road trip."

"Well, there's your answer, my friend. Report this incident to the United States police or see his father. I'm sure he wouldn't like this story to get out."

CHAPTER 5

Dream Holiday

On Friday, April 3, Daniel collected May from Koi Samui International Airport. Her beauty was just as he remembered; he hoped he could put aside everything that had happened over the past three weeks. May was equally happy to see him, happier now that her exams were behind her and she could concentrate on her new boyfriend. She greeted him with a shocked expression at how different he looked, with his weight loss and short hair. Daniel put it down to a healthy diet and frequent workouts at the gym; he certainty didn't want her to know about his excessive drug use, stress, and going days without eating.

After settling in at his bungalow, Daniel couldn't help but notice there was animosity between May and her mother. They were loving towards each other, like every other mother and daughter, but there was a secret between them, something they didn't want to share with him. He feared Phaung knew something about his relationship with Harrison. After three glorious days together, Daniel was still haunted by Harrison. He was on his mind constantly; what little sleep he had was interrupted by waking up sweating after countless nightmares. He came to the conclusion he needed to escape the resort and get as far away as possible. He suggested they take a vacation together, away from Thailand. At first, May was against this idea; for some reason, she wanted to stay close to her mother. When Phuang found out about this, she was furious; over a heated discussion with May, she insisted she go away with him.

On a beautiful sunny day, lying on the beach, Daniel stared down at May sunbathing and asked her where in the world would she want to go. Her first answer was England, where she'd love to find her father; otherwise, she'd always wanted to visit either New York, Dubai, or Sydney. Her dream would be to stay in a fabulous hotel in Dubai, wear beautiful clothes, and ride around in a chauffeur-driven limousine. She said this jokingly, knowing this dream would probably never happen. Daniel still wanted to impress her, and this gave him an idea. He left her sunbathing and disappeared with his MacBook to the reception lounge, for better wifi. He had an idea of an impressive hotel that would impress her; it was also the hotel himself wanted to stay at: the five-star Burj Al Arab, one of the world's most luxurious hotels.

After letting staff at the reception desk know when he'd be checking out, Daniel bumped into Dougie, the drug courier. He was in his tour-rep capacity and was able to spent time chatting. Daniel asked him if he had any contacts in Dubai.

Dougie laughed and said, "Of course. I know people that can get you anything, from drugs to prostitution. It's a strict police state, but there's serious money in Dubai, and there is nothing that money can't buy."

With this in mind, Daniel took his contact details, in case there was something he might desire whilst in Dubai.

May was ecstatic when he told her where they were going, although slightly bemused as to how he could afford such an extravagance. He also told her he needed to view business properties, which would be useful as an excuse if he needed to disappear from time to time, time on his own to ease an inner craving.

Phaung was emotional as they said their goodbyes; she waved them off with sadness in her eyes, as if she'd never see her daughter again. As they both sat in the first class seats of the Emirates Airbus 380, Daniel knew there was a hidden sadness between May and her mother. On a few occasions during the seven-hour flight, May had tears in her eyes. Daniel asked her why, with concern in his voice, but May insisted that everything was fine. On the shuttle bus from the jet to the terminal building, Daniel noticed a train of freight containers sporting the logo MGS (Messier Global Shipping). This made him wonder how large Harrison's father's company actually was, casting doubt in his mind that he could ever seek justice from such a powerful family.

They were collected from the airport by one of the hotel's white Rolls-Royce Phantoms; sitting side-by-side in the rear of the car, they nervously smiled at each other, overwhelmed with the extravagance of riding in such a beautiful car. May held his hand and thanked him for such a beautiful vacation; she reassured him that everything was okay. Daniel was happy, although still suspicious. After checking in at the Burj, they were taken to their panoramic suite and introduced to their own personal butler, who gave them a brief guided tour of their suite. May, who was determined to take advantage of his services, instructed him to run the jacuzzi and deliver chilled Champagne and canapés to their suite. As he left, closing the door behind him, Daniel and May both looked at each other and laughed, embarrassed by her demands.

After the jacuzzi, they lay on the bed in each other's arms. As May slept, Daniel lay awake, frustrated. This would be perfect if not for the living hell that was running through his mind, that living hell being still having thoughts for Harrison. He left May sleeping whilst he made a phone call to Dougie's contact. He knew now exactly what he wanted: something that would hopefully free him from his nightmares.

When May woke, they ordered room service; they were both still tired and certainly not in the mood to venture out to one of the hotel's restaurants. After they'd eaten, Daniel had another surprise for her: Tomorrow, they would be driven to the Wafi Mall, one of Dubai's largest shopping malls, for an extravagant spending spree. There she would be able to buy whatever clothes, shoes, and accessories her heart desired. At hearing this news, she put her hands over her face and cried with joy. This was all too much for her; she'd never seen such generosity. For the rest of the night at the luxurious hotel, they curled up on the huge sprawling sofa, wanting nothing more than to snuggle together, watch TV, and drink wine.

The next day, the chauffeur drove them to the mall. Daniel said he wanted to buy her a surprise, so they should separate. She agreed without any hesitation; they arranged to meet up at an Italian restaurant called Zucca's. He gave May his credit card and insisted she spend as much as she pleased. He needed to draw out a large amount of cash from a bank for the gift he wanted to buy her, and also to hand over to one of Dougie's contacts, who he'd arranged to meet at the mall.

About an hour before they'd planned to meet at the restaurant, May was having a cigarette outside a boutique. She spotted Daniel in the distance, sipping coffee. As she reached down to grab her bags to join him, she noticed he was now chatting to somebody, who then handed over an envelope to him. She thought it best not to disturb him and carried on shopping, sticking to the original meeting time. She arrived later at the restaurant, fully laden with designer bags from Prada, Gucci, and Versace. Daniel was standing outside, smoking and looking nervous, surrounded by his own bags from Ralph Lauren, Jaeger, and Hugo Boss. He made an excuse, complaining of an upset stomach, and suggested they have lunch back at the hotel. Daniel had learned that the restaurant didn't serve alcohol, and he desperately needed a drink.

That evening, whilst May was getting ready for dinner, Daniel video called Judith to show her around his luxurious hotel suite. As she looked with amazement at how beautiful it was, she couldn't help but worry that he was showing signs of compulsive spending. She remembered too well how her son would lavish money on designer goods as a form of therapy, to help ease a sadness he was feeling at the time. After his father died, he almost got himself into debt after endless extravagant spending sprees, buying designer clothes with department store cards.

This worry was fuelled when she spotted designer label carrier bags laid out on the sofa in the background. Whilst on the video call, she spoke to May for the first time; she was impressed by this beautiful, intelligent young lady who appeared to make her son very happy. After the call ended, May disappeared to the master bedroom upstairs to finish off getting ready.

After another hour had passed, May called Daniel from upstairs, telling him to close his eyes. He could hear her heels walking towards him down the curved staircase.

"You can open your eyes now," she said.

Daniel gasped with amazement at how fantastic she looked; she was wearing a black satin dress with ridiculously high heels.

"The dress is Versace, and the heels are Gucci," she said. "How do I look?"

"You look beautiful … But there's one thing missing."

She was confused by this until he took a gold necklace from his pocket. He led her to the mirror and stood behind her; she lifted her hair as he fastened the necklace.

"There you go; perfect!"

Looking at herself in the mirror, she whispered, "It's beautiful, so beautiful. Thank you."

She turned to kiss him and said she loved him.

Not expecting this, he paused for a second and then, with confidence, told her, "I love you too!"

After dinner, they drank cocktails at the hotel's sky-view bar. May became conscious of an Arab girl sitting at the next table, staring at her. She began to feel uncomfortable, believing the girl thought she was out of her depth at this hotel. When May left the table to use the washroom, the girl followed her; on their return, she and the girl were chatting like friends. May was overjoyed, Sophie had been admiring her dress and merely wanted to know where she'd bought it.

May invited Sophie and her husband Rashid to join them at their table. Daniel was slightly put out by this, but Sophie had a keen interest in Western fashion, and May loved the attention. Daniel nearly spat his cocktail out when Rashid told him he was an undercover officer for the UAE police force. As he stared into Rashid's pretty brown eyes, he joked to himself, thinking, *I suppose a line of coke and a quick fuck's out of the question?*

He didn't like Rashid; after telling him he renovated properties internationally, he kept asking questions about his work. Obviously, Daniel had absolutely no idea about property but managed to bluff every answer. As May talked clothes with Sophia, Rashid talked about his successful prosecutions on drugs; his last arrest was of a drug-addled male prostitute. The conversation turned to homosexuality and how the victim of a male rape could also be prosecuted under UAE law for having sex with another man, even though nonconsenual. Daniel was fascinated by this, although deeply disturbed. Daniel and May made their excuses to turn in for the night; both had drank too much and wanted time alone together.

In the elevator, May whispered seductively into Daniel's ear, "Just wait till you see the lingerie I bought from Agent Provocateur. I can't wait for you to remove them. Did you see Sophie looking at my breasts? I think she liked them. I think she wanted to touch them; I would have liked her to touch them."

May smiled as Daniel held his suit jacket to cover his erection, which showed through his trousers. As the elevator door opened, May took off her heels and ran giggling back to the suite.

The next morning, Daniel lay awake, dreading the coming day. He wondered if he was doing the right thing. All he knew was that he needed to try something, anything, to heal the wounds in his mind and take control of his life again. Over breakfast, May mentioned that Sophie and Rashid would be joining them at the indoor pool this morning.

She also asked, "Do you think Sophie knows Rashid is gay?"

"Rashid's gay?"

"Seriously, Daniel, you didn't know?"

"I had no idea. How did you know?"

"It was obvious. I studied him. I followed his eyes. I saw the way he looked at you; he likes you! Why do you think he constantly mentioned homosexuals? He was testing the water with you. Remember, Daniel, I worked in a hotel in Bangkok, where I saw many of these supposedly happy married Arab couples."

Daniel sat looking bemused, wondering if perhaps he should have a little fun with this sanctimonious hypocrite. Maybe he should try to seduce him. *Perfect,* he thought. This might take his mind off what he'd planned for today.

After breakfast, they both luxuriated on loungers at the indoor swimming pool, still slightly delicate from last night's cocktails. They lay back peacefully, admiring the magnificent décor. At ten, Rashid and Sophie waved whilst making their way to join them. Sophie asked a worker to bring over two more loungers and instructed him to place hers close to May. She and May flicked through beauty and fashion magazines as Daniel went to shower before having a swim. On his return, still dripping wet, he stood at the side of the pool, where Rashid was lying, his wet shorts almost transparent. He'd strategically placed his semi-erect penis down his opposite dress side, to emphasise its size. Then after tucking both thumbs into his Burberry shorts, pulling them down slightly just beneath his pubic hair line, he shook his wet hands over Rashid's body, asking, "Are you coming in? You coming for a swim, Rash?"

Rashid was embarrassed and afraid that Sophie and May were aware of what sight was pleasing his eyes; he quickly got up and jumped into the pool. After a brief swim, May brought over two glasses of orange juice and placed them on the edge of the pool behind Rashid's head. He was supporting his body weight in the deep water with his arms on the edge and his back to the swimming-pool wall. Daniel thanked May and swam under water towards Rashid; as he floated to the surface, he then reached for his juice, briefly brushing his torso and groin up against Rashid's.

As he drank his juice, Daniel looked down into the water, smiling at Rashid's now fully erect penis trying to force its way out his tight blue Lycra trunks. Daniel turned and sniggered to himself, pleased at what he'd achieved. His seduction technique had been a success. Depending on how his business meeting went later, he might take his advances a step further tonight.

Rashid didn't talk much after getting out of the pool; he lay on his lounger, looking frustrated and sorry for himself. Sophie didn't stop talking to draw a breath; even May, with the patience of a saint, was growing tired of her. It was now twelve o'clock. Daniel apologised and made his excuses to leave; he needed to get showered and changed for his business meeting at two o'clock. He'd told May he was viewing property for sale.

In the suite, Daniel poured himself a large vodka and tonic to drink whilst getting ready. As he started to strip for the shower, May ran into the suite, looking for a cigarette. She grabbed his drink and took a large mouthful.

Daniel looked puzzled and asked, "Where's Rash and Sophie?"

"Sophie's booking treatments for us in the spa; as for Rashid, he might have himself arrested for having immoral thoughts about sex with another man, or he's probably masturbating at the sight of your cock in those wet shorts earlier. I'd go for the latter."

"You make me laugh. I love you so much!"

"Seriously, Daniel, you're such a tease with him. I'm starting to get jealous; he saw more of your cock today than I have. When Sophie felt the fabric on my bikini top, her little finger brushed against my nipple, causing it to become erect. I watched as she squeezed her legs tightly together. I thought she was about to have an orgasm, but it wasn't my nipple she getting excited about. It was my Mon Cheri bikini. I'll send her into full outer space orgasm tonight, when I wear my Stella McCartney for dinner."

Daniel laughed as he stood, naked, ready for his shower. May held his penis and begged him to not go to his business appointment. He looked into her face, pushing her hair back affectionately and saying, "This viewing is very important. It's vital I go. My … our future depends on this."

At the hotel entrance, May waved goodbye to her handsome, well-dressed boyfriend, believing he was just about to score a prospective business deal. He waved back her, looking terrified, like a soldier about to go into battle. As the chauffeur opened the rear door of the white Rolls-Royce Phantom, Daniel gracefully stepped and told the chauffeur the address of his destination. The driver looked slightly puzzled as to why a guest at the Berg Al Arab would be visiting nothing more than a building site. As the white Phantom floated though the busy streets of Dubai, Daniel looked out of the window, nervously dreading reaching his destination. For once, his mind was fixated with fear.

When he reached his destination, he instructed the chauffeur to collect him in exactly one hour's time. As he stepped out from the car, his eyes were drawn upwards to the height of the imposing high-rise office building, windowless and only half-complete. A security guard, who'd been expecting him, opened the gates. Daniel was now crippled with fear, as the guard strode hastily towards him. Standing at what looked like seven feet tall, he towered over him, introducing himself as Hassan. He smiled, revealing yellow teeth, whilst wiping sweat away from his forehead. As he turned to lead the way to the building entrance, Daniel turned his head away to avoid the stench of body odour. He was a complete contrast to the well-groomed, smart Arab men he'd become accustomed to at the hotel. He spoke very good English, though, as he gave directions to the floor his business meeting was on. He secretly passed Daniel a packet of cigarettes, and with his hand on his shoulder, he pushed him away.

Daniel reached the third floor, out of breath after climbing the stairs in the intense hot air (the elevators were yet to be installed). He followed the corridor to the first large room on the right; in there was a doorway to another room. He tossed his bag on the floor and inspected the contents of the cigarette packet; a small pack of cocaine was in it. On a makeshift workbench, he took out his wallet and laid out a line on a credit card. After a large snort, he closed his eyes. His head seemed to spin 360 degrees and then rotated like a helicopter blade. His feet almost rose off the ground; the effect was almost immediate. When he opened his eyes, his body lowered to the floor, he now had the confidence to face what was about to happen.

There in front of him stood a construction worker, who looked Pakistani. He was wearing dirty blue overalls standing at the entrance to the adjoining room, his face raging with anger. He slowly walked towards Daniel. When he reached him, he spat on the floor in front of him and then threw a fist into Daniel's face, knocking him backwards into the arms of a second man, who then threw a sack over his head. The second man pulled the sack over his shoulders and tied a rope around his arms to restrict his movements. The first man then kicked him to the ground and stood back to allow the second man to continue kicking him.

At this point, Daniel didn't scream or shout for help; he just lay face down, shaking with fear. The men looked at each other; they seemed indecisive as to what they should do next. The first man nodded as if to give the go-ahead for the second man to remove his trousers.

When his trousers were pulled down to his ankles, Daniel started to scream, "Enough! Stop, please! No, please stop!"

The men looked at each other, both smiling, until the second opened his overalls and took out his penis. As he began to insert it into his rectum, Daniel wriggled and started screaming for help again.

Suddenly, Hassan ran into the room and walked over to the men in a rage, instructing them to leave Daniel alone.

When the men disappeared, Hassan wrapped tape around his mouth to silence his screams and stood back, watching him wriggle on the floor whilst lighting a cigarette. After he'd finished his cigarette, he started to untie him; when he was freed, Hassan passed him a bottle of water and a tissue for his cut lip.

"Thank you. I didn't think they were going to stop."

"Mr Reed, I'm afraid to tell you I instructed them both to sodomise you and leave you for dead; they had no idea that you were the client, and you shouting 'Stop' or 'Enough' would make them do so. You paid me good money for this treatment. I wanted to make it as real as possible. I gagged you with tape, just to add a little extra fear, and sir, you were screaming quite loudly."

Daniel laughed and then almost broke into tears as he struggled in pain to stand up. Hassan helped him to his feet and walked him to his bag; inside, he had identical clothes to what he was wearing, which he threw into a garbage bag.

"Mr Reed, you are my second male client; my first wanted to be raped as a form of sexual gratification. Tell me, why would you want to inflict such fear and pain on yourself?"

"I wanted to be in control. I wanted to be able to say 'Stop!' I wanted to be able to make the assault end. I wanted to inflict fear and pain on myself as a form of punishment, of feeling for someone I don't want wish to have feelings for!"

On his return to the hotel, Daniel undressed in front of the bathroom mirror; with a feeling of achievement in pain, he examined his bruised body. With a cut lip and a black eye, he looked at his reflection, now fearing his own sanity. He could hear May entering the suite and shouted his name. He forced a fake smile upon himself and called to let her know where he was. As she entered the room, her joyful face quickly turned to a startled expression at the sight of Daniel's bruised and battered body. He smiled and reassured her that he'd been stupid: He'd taken a tumble down a flight of stairs, blaming the vodka and extreme heat; apart from his stupidity, he'd had a successful day and wanted to celebrate.

May was undecided if this story was true, but she didn't question him any further, for fear of angering him. To his annoyance, May had arranged to have dinner with Rashid and Sophie at one of the hotel's restaurants. Daniel asked if she could change plans and have dinner served in their suite; with his bruised and cut face, he didn't want to be seen in public.

Before getting ready for dinner, they relaxed in the jacuzzi, sipping Champagne. May seductively caressed her foot between his legs; she looked puzzled when he just stared into space, oblivious to her intentions.

"Where do you go to, my love?"

Not answering, he continued in his own world. She moved around the tub to sit next to him, stroking his hair back as he looked up to the ceiling.

"My mother used to say my head was always high in the clouds," he replied. "I like being high, and sometimes, my head drifts away within the clouds."

He turned to her and said, "I was just thinking, May, I was thinking I'm looking forward to spending the rest of my life with you."

She kissed him whilst her hand slowly caressed his penis; she masturbated him slowly until he reached orgasm. She watched his facial reaction as he climaxed; as tears fell from his eyes, he looked sad, tormented by a grief she wished he'd share with her.

At seven o'clock, the butler answered the door to greet their guests, Rashid and Sophie. Sophie looked stunning; against Rashid's wishes, she was wearing a fashionable (and revealing) Western dress. May also looked stunning in her short Stella McCartney dress. It was obvious Rashid was in a furious mood: furious at Sophie's disrespect towards their strict Muslim religion and furious with May for encouraging her.

They'd organised a Cantonese banquet to be brought to the suite and served at their candlelit dining table. Rashid avoided making any eye contact with Daniel, uncomfortable knowing he knew his secret, a secret he himself felt disgusted by. Daniel sensed how uncomfortable he felt; he thrived on making him feel even more uncomfortable by talking about his uncle Hugo and his young black boyfriend. May then mentioned her uncle Sirichai, who was also gay, bringing Rashid to an uncomfortable silence. The next topic of conversation was that he and Sophie were trying for a baby. Daniel seethed with the thought of this condescending, hypocritical jerk reproducing.

As the butler set the table, Daniel was starting his third bottle of wine. It was clearly obvious to Sophie and May that Daniel and Rashid were never going to see eye to eye. As they talked amongst themselves, they overheard Daniel mention how he used to take cocaine and smoke pot. May, who was anti-drugs, glared at him at this revelation. She hastily took Sophie to the master bedroom upstairs to show her designer clothes collection, leaving the boys to out-stare each other across the table, with mutual dislike.

Daniel reached for the last of his cocaine and chopped up a line, to the disgust of Rashid, who snarled, "You better stop that. You stop that now! I must warn you of the consequences of being in possession of that substance."

Daniel smiled as he snorted his line. Rashid stood up quickly, knocking his chair over. Daniel walked around to his side of the table whilst unbuttoning his shirt. When he reached him, his shirt was now fully open. He leant into his face whilst staring into his eyes, breathing heavily. Rashid looked terrified, almost shaking with fear, as Daniel moved his lips towards his. His hand reached down to unbutton his trousers. As Daniel reached for his erect penis, Rashid's eyes rolled back into his head; he started to moan and quiver. Daniel looked at him, concerned; at first, he thought he was having a fit, although it wasn't a fit. He was having an orgasm and ejaculated into Daniel's hand.

Rashid looked terrified, yet relieved, Daniel looked at him, puzzled, wondering if perhaps this was Rashid's first sexual encounter with another man. He looked at him with sympathy that at the age of thirty-two, Rashid had experienced a lifetime of sexual frustration and denial. As Daniel walked backwards whilst buttoning his shirt, he could see Sophie standing at the top of the stairs, with her hand over her mouth, watching them. Distraught at what she'd seen, she ran to the door to leave the suite. Rashid stood staring at Daniel, looking like a broken man.

"Are you satisfied now, Daniel, is this what you wanted? You're free to do whatever you choose in your country. We are not as lucky; there are laws here. Perhaps you should take a long look in the mirror. What's your excuse for being a hypocrite?"

Daniel thought to himself for just that moment; everything became clear to him. He knew he was right. He grabbed Rashid's shoulder, begging for his forgiveness and explaining that his head had been muddled now for some time, and his judgement cloudy.

"I forgive you, Daniel, but I don't think you forgive yourself! I don't think you even like yourself; perhaps you should go to May now and be truthful with her."

After Rashid left, Daniel stood staring up towards the master bedroom, convincing himself that now was the time to tell her everything. He walked up the stairs, dreading what to expect. As he slowly opened the door, he saw May curled up on the bed in the foetal position, crying. Convinced that she'd seen what had happened, he stroked her hair, comforting her and apologising.

In tears, she turned to him and said, "Sirichai's just called me; my mother's too sick to work. It's started, Daniel; she's dying! Three months ago, she was told her cancer was terminal and was given six, maybe twelve months. She was determined to work up till the day she could no longer do so. That day is now!"

Suddenly, it became clear why Phaung was off work due to sickness, why she collapsed, and why she looked so tired and frail. Phaung had given

Sirichai strict instructions, telling May not to rush home to Thailand. She was a proud woman and did not wish to be a burden on anybody, especially her daughter. She didn't want May fussing at her bedside, instead of enjoying her new life with Daniel, which was why she insisted she go on vacation with him. As much as May wanted to respect her wishes, she told Daniel she wanted to fly back to Thailand tomorrow.

Daniel was relieved that May didn't know about Rashid but saddened about Phaung, Still high from his line of coke and struggling to concentrate, he successfully managed to call the airline to book seats on the first flight back to Thailand the next morning.

After a sleepless night, worrying that he could have lost her, Daniel stood looking angrily at the lady at the check-out desk, wishing she would hurry, in fear of bumping into either Rashid or Sophie. He was dreading any form confrontation or anything that would upset May further. May had enquired why they both left so abruptly. Daniel told her that Sophie had found them in a heated discussion, almost fighting; she thought it best for them to leave.

Just as the chauffeur opened the car door, Sophie ran out from the hotel's main door, waving at May. She told Daniel to wait in the car, for she wanted to say goodbye to her properly. Daniel was panicking, insisting she simply wave goodbye, worried that they'd miss their flight.

May was having none of it and jumped out to talk to her. Daniel sat patiently, dreading the worst; he started sweating. Whilst wiping his forehead, he asked to chauffeur to turn up the air conditioner and watched with fear as their conversation turned into an argument.

May made her way back to the car, looking angry. She didn't wait for the door to be opened; she climbed into the back of the car and held Daniel's hand furiously, ordering the chauffeur to drive away.

"What did you talk about?" he asked. "You looked like you were arguing."

"I don't wish to talk about her, stupid, silly girl! She's not important."

It wasn't until May had a few drinks on the flight that she spoke about their conversation. Sophie had said that Daniel had encouraged Rashid to taking cocaine with him before making a homosexual pass at her husband. May was furious with her, calling her disillusioned and vindictive. She also said her fictitious lies were brought on by Daniel unknowingly flirting with him and mentioning he once used cocaine. This came as a relief to Daniel. He laughed about the consequences of being in possession in the UAE. Why would he want to make a pass at a police officer?

May slept in his comforting arms throughout the rest of the flight; all he could think about was how lucky he was to have her, how precious she was. His main priority from now was to be there for her. It was time to put those demons in his head to rest and concentrate solely on the person he loved, the precious person in his arms.

CHAPTER 6

A New High

Sirichai collected them from Surat Thani International Airport, on the western shore of the Gulf of Thailand. It was a one-hour drive to Phaung's home in Don Sak, but it felt like a lifetime, travelling in Sirichai's battered old Nissan Micra. Sirichai was in his late forties; he worked on the ferry to Koi Samui and was a kind man, always smiling and happy. May adored him. The house was just as May had described: a tiny one-story, two-bedroom house with a veranda full of beautiful potted flowers. Phaung was sleeping when they arrived, due to the amount of painkillers she needed to take. When she woke, she was delighted to see her daughter but upset they'd cut short their vacation for her.

Daniel was made to feel extremely welcome. Sirichai offered his bedroom to him and he'd take the sofa, but Daniel was hearing nothing of this. He politely declined his offer and suggested he rent a room nearby, somewhere he and May could spend time alone together. This came as a relief for May, who hadn't lived at home for three years and was used to her own space and independence. She remembered her school friend's parents let out cabins and huts in a secluded forest near Nang Kam Beach; she suggested driving him there tomorrow.

May drove him there early the next morning in the ageing Micra. Daniel held on for dear life on the steep winding mountain tracks up to the cabins. The tracks were lined with sinister concrete statues of bizarre-looking people and animals, which gave the forest an eerie feel. Because May was a friend of the family, they were given one of the better cabins at a reasonable rate. Their cabin was secluded from the other tourists, except for their neighbour, Eliot, who was a permanent resident. He was a friendly, sandal-wearing hippy in his sixties, sporting a long scraggily beard and looking permanently stoned.

The cabin was perfect, apart from the view of Koi Samui, which Daniel thought would be a constant reminder of the resort. Realising they could be in Don Sak for some time, he decided to buy a car. He struck upon the idea to put the car in Sirichai's name, making it easier for documentation and insurance for himself and May. When the time came for them to move on again, he'd simply hand the car over to him as a token of good will. He bought a second-hand Lexus 4x4 at a very low price, this being an ideal vehicle for the forest tracks.

For the first few weeks, he enjoyed his independence and being alone during the day. His evenings were spent with May at the cabin. He was beginning to feel worthy of himself again, not wanting to punish himself with self-destruction.

Here was his daily routine:

05.30. Drive May to her mother's house; drink tea with Phaung; and chat with Sirichai before he left for work.

06.45. Kiss May goodbye and drive to Surat Thani.

07.50. Arrive at Sculpture's gym, pre-workout cigarette before entering.

10.15. After first workout, essential cigarette and energy drink break whilst flirting with eighteen-year-old identical twin models, Kamnan and Sunti.

12.00. Leave gym exhausted; his body was getting into good shape. The twins asked Daniel if he'd like to get high with them followed by a threesome; he was flattered by their offer, but he declined and went for lunch instead.

13.20. Walk off lunch around the city shops and look for a nice gift for May. Venture into Tops market and shop for fresh vegetables and meat for whatever May wants to cook for dinner.

15.00. Call into Wang Tai Hotel for free Wi-Fi; relax over two large, refreshing beers.

16.30. Drive back to Don Sak and look forward to seeing May.

17.40. Drink wine on the veranda whilst May cooks dinner for everybody. Sirichai arrives back from work; his turn to care for Phaung.

19.00. Make our way back to the cabin, where we eat together and drink wine, sitting outside and watching the sun set. Comfort her, care for her, be there for her, and hopefully make love to her.

Daniel even rekindled his friendship with Auguste, chatting to him daily online, both promising they'd meet up again soon. Apart from sharing the occasional joint with Eliot, he had no interest in binge drinking or getting wasted on drugs; however, things started to change for the worst as Phaung's health deteriorated.

When she could no longer to eat, wash, or use the bathroom by herself, Phaung became angry and aggressive with May; losing her pride and dignity devastated her. She hated being fully reliant on her daughter; one day, she refused to eat and threw a bowl of hot soup over May, and then she cried at what she'd done, begging her daughter to put a pillow over her head and end her misery. This took its toll on May's sanity. She never showed how upset she was front of her mother; instead, she'd save these feelings until she was back at the cabin, where she'd take her frustrations out on Daniel. Instead of bringing them closer, it was pushing them apart.

Gone were the romantic meals watching the sunset and then making love; instead, she'd arrive back at the cabin and drink heavily. She herself would also become unreasonable and abusive, envious of his carefree lifestyle, completely oblivious to the fact that he was still wrestling with his own demons. This made Daniel feel lonely and isolated; he felt hopeless and unnecessary. He needed an escape.

He seized his opportunity to escape one day when Sirichai had planned to go for drinks after work with friends. May had agreed to sleep over that night, leaving Daniel to his own devices. His plan was to go to Sculptures as usual and then call Dougie to arrange a meet with a recommended dealer. That morning, he dropped May off as usual and went for a workout at the gym. His plan was to meet the supplier in the afternoon and then get wired back at the cabin.

After his workout, he decided to use the steam room; on a few occasions before, the twins had followed him in, looking for sex. Daniel would always immediately walk straight out, embarrassed. He never felt comfortable in such a small, hot environment, especially sitting next to two naked brothers, but today was different.

He leaned back and relaxed, closing his eyes whilst sweat poured out from every pore. Suddenly, he heard the door open; with one eye slightly open, he could see it was the twins. Both sat on either side of him. On this occasion, they didn't speak, almost as if they knew he was theirs for the taking, like he'd finally given into their demands for sex. Even though the idea of sex with two identical twins was appealing, he was here for one reason: He was here for the high. Slowly, each brother gently stroked his inner thigh as they kissed and caressed his shoulders. Daniel started to panic; the intense heat and close confinement was too much for him to bear. He needed to get out.

Outside the gym, he lit a cigarette, knowing they'd shortly follow. He knew damn well what answer he'd give if they were to invite him back to get high. It wasn't long before he was following them on foot, through backstreets stinking of rotten food and sewage, in search of a fix. Their apartment was only a ten-minute walk away. It wasn't the most pleasant of dwellings. Inside was like a bedsit, nothing more than a pile of unwashed plates and a fridge, classed as a kitchen area; in the corner was a large double bed with stained, unwashed sheets. Daniel was shocked at how two people who kept themselves looking immaculate could live in such a cockroach-infested rathole.

Sunti played hip-hop ridiculously loud and opened the fridge in search of beers. Kamnan took his vest off and reached for his crack pipe from behind the microwave. Daniel had never done crack cocaine before and was slightly apprehensive at first, but this was a whole new experience, an experience he was eager to try. As Kemnan heated the rock, Daniel threw a large bundle of bills on the kitchen table, asking them to follow his instructions. He reached his hand out of the window to untie a cord from a makeshift washing line; both twins looked puzzled as to what he could possible need it for. Sunti had sensed that Daniel was stressed. He sat on the bed, patting his hand to where he wanted Daniel to sit, so he could massage his shoulders. He did this without hesitation as Kemnan kneeled in front of him. Whilst lifting his T-shirt off, he slid the pipe into his mouth before he started to pull his shorts down to his ankles to give him oral pleasure.

The high after the first hit was immense; the euphoria and sexual desire was almost immediate. He also felt the desire to be punished and abused; he demanded they both force their way inside him and for them to cause him as much pain as physically possible. He handed the cord to Sunti, who was sitting behind him, and told him to tie his arms behind his back. Sunti tied his arms tight together and passed the remaining cord to Kemnan, who was on his knees in order for him to tie his legs together. After a while, he passed out.

He woke at 18.30 to sound of his phone ringing; he was lying on his stomach on the bed, looking through the window at an old lady singing whilst cooking in the apartment opposite. He remembered how his mum would sing along to songs played on the radio when she'd cook him breakfast. On this occasion, he wasn't waking up to the smell of a cooked breakfast; he was rising to the pungent smell of burnt plastic, the almost chemical smell of crack cocaine. Oh, how he missed his mum: her dreadful singing, her perfume, and her comforting him when things were bad.

Kemnan had started smoking once again; the tiny fan was blowing the smell towards where Daniel was lying. He felt sick, terrified to move for fear of vomiting. Kemnan was sitting naked on the floor, rocking backwards and forwards, chanting like a drug-addled lunatic. This dampened the temptation to smoke more crack, although the temptation was great. The come-down feeling was worse than any amount of cocaine he'd taken in the past. He felt suicidal, but after being sick, being sick was the priority. He couldn't face the bathroom; he scrambled to get dressed and made a quick exit. Just as he opened the door, Sunti ran from bathroom and handed him two small tubes of a gel-like substance.

"Thank you for the money, Daniel. Here, for you. Have a good trip!"

He grabbed the tubes and left. Just before he unlocked the car door, he threw up in the parking lot; this came as such a relief! He was now free to get back to the cabin and clean himself up, although the feeling of depression was almost unbearable. Still high and confused, he took a different route up to the cabin, one which he was unfamiliar with. It was steeper, with sharper bends than the usual way. With tears in his eyes, he put his foot down, driving faster and faster, not caring if he crashed.

When he reached a dead end at the highest point, there was nothing: no cabins. He was completely lost. He leant his head on the steering wheel, wishing he didn't exist anymore. He suddenly remembered the tubes Sunti gave him and wondered if they'd cure the misery in his soul. With one mouthful, the two tubes were gone. Almost by magic, his head slowly became clear again. He smiled as he put the car into drive and put his foot down again, hurtling down the tight hairpin bends.

When he eventually found the correct route, May called. She was upbeat today and said she missed him and looked forward to seeing him tomorrow. Daniel was his happy self again, until he drove past the statues. A statue of a suited man turned his head as he drove by. Daniel slammed his brakes on; in the rear view mirror, the statue was now staring at his car. Daniel was now pleasantly high; he smiled and drove on to the cabin.

After locking the Lexus, he walked up to open the cabin door. A voice from behind him called out his name. He recognised the voice and turned slowly, fearing who it might be. It was his dad, Graham, sitting in the driver's seat of a car. Daniel tightened his lip and turned to walk away; he wasn't in the mood to take abuse from him today.

"Dan, Dan … You not saying hello to your old man?"

Daniel's hand was trembling as he struggled to put the key in the door, with his heart pounding.

"I see you're spending the money I left you wisely, the same money I works hard for. You're full of surprises, son! Not even I thought you could stoop so low as to pay a couple of Pakkies to beat you up. And seriously, you just paid for two ladyboys to bumfuck you! What's your problem with the American boy? I thought you queers liked that kind of thing? Your mum will be so proud of you, Dan!"

Daniel turned and walked angrily to the car; he snapped, "Shouldn't you be busy rotting in hell, Dad?"

He looked at him with disgust before turning and walking away again.

Graham leaned his head out of the window and shouted, "Dan, Dan, I've got some of your new friends in the car. I bet they're really pleased to have had you as a friend. Come see, Dan! I dare you, son."

He walked slowly to the car, dreading what he might see inside. In the rear seat was a corpse in a body bag; he opened the door and reached for the zip. His hand trembled with fear, terrified of who he might see inside; he

66

couldn't open it. Graham shouted abuse, calling him gutless and ordering him to see who was in the boot. As he walked around to the rear of the car, the boot began to open. Daniel screamed out with fear, with his hand over his mouth, at the sight that lay before him. It was himself, dead, curled up in the boot. His eyes were wide open, with a pale blue complexion; his wrists were bandaged in blood-soaked dressings.

Graham screamed at him once again, "This is your fate; this is what will become of you!"

He walked backwards away from the car, only to scream once again in shock. It was Eliot.

"Calm down, calm down, kid. What's up with you? Have you forgotten your groceries?" he said jokingly at the sight of Daniel staring into an empty boot.

Daniel looked once again, only this time, it was empty. Eliot told him he was only having a bad trip and escorted him back to the cabin. As he passed the car, Graham was still sitting at the wheel. He held his hand through the window in the shape of a gun, just like Parker at the resort.

Eliot returned to his cabin an hour later to check on him. Daniel was now sitting naked on his bed, having a pleasant conversation about domestic pets in the UK. He was having this conversation with a wooden sculpture of a dhole, an Asiatic wild cat. Eliot stood at the door, struggling not to laugh, more still when Daniel politely excused himself to the dhole, explaining he had more pressing matters with Jesus. Jesus, who saw this as an open invitation to make him look even more ridiculous, told him the statues had requested his company. Eliot knew he too had had many debates with the statues whilst under the influence of mind-enhancing substances; he took a seat outside the cabin and watched with amusement as Daniel wandered towards his spiritual calling.

The first statue to greet him was an old Thai lady, who spoke with knowledge and authority. She warned him of the consequences of seeking revenge and seeking closure, advising him to find this in his own mind first.

A statue of a war hero with an arm missing was the second to speak; he rudely interrupted, insisting he didn't need to listen to the old lady. His advice was completely the opposite: With his only arm, he pointed to the statue that had turned its head to him earlier. He spoke aggressively with bitterness and rage, advising not to dwell on past wrongdoings, to face his fear head on, and to seek revenge, whatever the consequences.

Daniel covered his ears at the sound of their loud bickering and walked towards the statue, now knowing who it might be.

The statue was of Harrison; he was smartly dressed in a suit and tie. He stood motionless, looking down at Daniel with tears in his eyes. Daniel looked at him with sympathy and asked why he was crying. There was no response, no explanation. Suddenly, the Thai lady shouted, "Car! Back into positions!"

He could see headlights in the distance, making their way up the track. Daniel quickly stood next to Harrison and formed a statue-like pose, convinced he'd go unnoticed. The car was filled with heavily stoned backpackers, laughing as they drove past. The driver slammed on his brakes before reversing back to where Daniel was standing, completely naked. Each of the passengers looked in disbelief before one jumped out and taunted him by tweaking his nose. Failing to make him move, he urinated against his leg, causing an uproar of laughter from the car. Even this failed to get a reaction; he then stood staring into Daniel's eyes in shock as to how much he was out of it. As they drove away, one by one, each statue began to laugh; even Harrison turned to him and smiled. Totally oblivious to why they found this so amusing, he wandered back to the cabin to where Jesus was waiting at the door for him.

In the morning, he woke up, laying on his side, staring at the dirty footmarks on the floor without any recollection about yesterday. The room was filled with cigarette smoke; his mobile rang. It was May; she'd called to ask if she could use the Lexus to run some errands and if he would watch Phaung whilst she was out. He agreed, telling her he'd be there as soon as possible. Just as he finished the call, he realised where the smoke was coming from: It was Eliot, who was lying next to him in bed. Shocked, he jumped out of bed, covering himself with a towel.

"Ha ha, you don't remember anything, do you?"

"What the hell happened last night?"

"I found you yesterday, throwing up, stinking of crack; you'd just been having a slanging match with the invisible man sitting in your car. It looked like you were having a bad LSD trip. You then went on to talk to the statues after giving a poor dhole nightmares about the Alsatian dog you had as pet as a child."

"You and me, we didn't …, did we?" Daniel asked sheepishly.

"Ha ha, no, we didn't; you asked me, but I'm not way inclined that way. I slept with you in case you went wandering off again. Now then, you go and shower; go to your pretty girlfriend. I'll clean up here."

When he arrived at the house, his head was still in bits. The drugs from yesterday were still messing with his mind. May was sitting on the veranda, waiting for him; she'd made a special effort today with her appearance, wearing a dress and make-up. She looked her usual, beautiful self. Even in his confused state of mind, it was clear to him she needed a break from her caring duties, and he was more than happy to help her out. It wasn't long after she left when Phaung called out for him to sit with her. When he entered her room, he was shocked at how much her health had deteriorated since he'd seen her last week. She slept most of the time, but on this occasion, she was wide awake and wanted to talk. Her speech was slurred but fully coherent; she held him by the hand and asked him to sit next to her on the bed.

"Daniel, there's something I need to tell you. I know what that American boy did to you, and I'm so sorry. I was powerless to help. Parker threatened me; he said if I spoke up about it, he'd make serious problems for May in Bangkok. He said he'd set her up in possession of drugs and get her locked up in prison for the rest of her life.

"Parker works for the boy's father as his bodyguard; his job is to protect him and keep him out of trouble. Instead of doing his job properly, on the night it happened, he was with a girl. Her name is Sai Meesanang; she works at the resort as a maid. It was she who told me about his true identity. She'd overheard a phone call with Parker, talking to Mr Fisher, begging him to keep his job. He promised he'd cover up what Harrison had done. He of course lied as to why he wasn't doing his job properly; he would have certainly lost his job if Mr Fisher knew he was with a prostitute."

Tears began to fall from his eyes as Phuang fell into another deep sleep; he thanked her and promised he would always love and protect her daughter, vowing she would have a beautiful life. Whilst he was in the kitchen making coffee, he stared out the window with anger. This anger was now for Parker as much as for Harrison; he vowed to himself he'd never inflict harm on himself again and that he would seek revenge.

Two days later, Phaung died peacefully, with both Daniel and May at her bedside. Sirichai rushed home from work, but it was too late for him to say goodbye to his beloved sister. That night at Phaung's house, May fell asleep in the sitting room, leaving Daniel to finish off a bottle of vodka by himself. It had been a stressful day, and he thought to himself that he deserved it.

After falling asleep, he woke suddenly to a chill through his spine. Half-asleep, his eyes barely open, he watched Phaung slowly walk into the room, almost gliding, feet barely touching the floor. She went over to May, brushed her hair back from her face, smiled, and kissed her goodbye. After pulling up her blanket to her shoulders to tuck her in, she turned and headed back towards the door, barely acknowledging Daniel, who was also in the room.

He whispered quietly, "Do I get a goodbye from you, Phaung?"

There was no answer from her; she briefly turned to him, looking distraught with tears in her eyes, and shook her head. Her face full of sadness, she quickly turned away again, afraid to look at him. After he fell asleep again, he dreamed of being led up a large staircase in an old house. His feet were barely touching the floor. He was walking up the stairs to a bright light, in peace, and he calmly walked up to his destiny.

This dream puzzled him the next day; he wasn't sure if what he'd seen was just a dream or another hallucination. It worried him that Phaung seemed to be upset with him; he wished she'd said goodbye, and he wished he hadn't caused her any problems when she was so ill. In a positive frame of mind, he knew that he couldn't go back and change the past, only concentrate on the future, a future with May.

The evening after Phaung's funeral, Daniel and May enjoyed a picnic on Nang Kam Beach, at exactly the same spot where Phaung used to take her as a child. They feasted on mini fish cakes, fried wontons, and chicken satay sticks, drinking wine and sitting on a blanket in front of a campfire.

As the sun was setting over Koi Samui islands, they toasted Phaung's life with Champagne, May wanted to celebrate her mother's life, not to mourn her death. Wearing just shorts and a T-shirt, she asked Daniel to close his eyes and played him a ballad by his favourite artist, Ed Sheeran. When she asked him to open them, she was standing in front of him, wearing the same Versace dress he'd bought her in Dubai. Without any make-up or jewellery, she looked even more beautiful, standing barefoot in the sand with the sun setting behind her. He got to his feet, and they held each other and danced slowly together in each other's arms. This seemed the right moment for Daniel's proposal.

"I love you, May," he began. "I want to spend the rest of my life with you. Come to America with me; we can do a road trip together. Starting in New York, we can travel down to the Deep South and then work our way up to the West Coast. After getting married in Las Vegas, we could return to the UK to find your father."

May stood back and looked at him with a shocked expression.

"Excuse me? What did you say?"

"I'm sorry, I'm jumping ahead here. Oh yes, I forgot to ask: Will you marry me?"

She put both hands over her mouth as tears of happiness fell from her eyes.

"Yes, yes, I will marry you. I love you, Daniel!"

CHAPTER 7

Seeking Justice

STOPOn the long, eighteen-hour flight to New York, in between the occasional nap, Daniel listened to music on his headphones. May was sitting in between him and a friendly American lady called Marianne. Marianne had bought large selection of magazines to read throughout the flight. May was more than happy to help her sort through this huge selection of fashion and celebrity gossip reading material. Daniel closed his eyes and enjoyed his music whilst sipping wine; every now and again, he was disturbed by May, who was getting too excited at pictures of Hollywood A-list actresses wearing a certain dress and discussing it with Marianne.

He was happy in his own little world of music and alcohol. He'd stopped taking his headphone off and pretending to be interested in another juicy celebrity headline; that was, up until Marianne showed him a picture of Harrison Fisher and his soon-to-be-wife, Susan, looking loved up as they watched a baseball game. The caption read:

"Troubled tycoon's son happy after another stint in rehab for depression; looking forward to marrying his long-term girlfriend, Susan Wallace."

Not believing his eyes, he ripped his earphones off and asked if he could read it properly. He sat there, trying to act calm, reading every sickly word praising the beast, his hands shaking and seething with anger. His heart was racing. He felt faint; his vision became blurred, and he struggled to breathe. He needed to leave his seat in search for the privacy of the washroom. As he stood up, his legs struggled to walk properly, as if they were unable to carry his weight. As he struggled along the aisle, he felt as if all the passengers knew what had happened to him and were now judging him; they seemed to stare at him in disapproval and disgust. Struggling to breathe, he clutched every seat as a guide to help him walk.

In the washroom, he took deep breaths in the hope of calming himself down; he remembered how his mum would tell him to breathe in through the nose and out through the mouth. As he began to breathe properly again, he stared at himself in the mirror, when an idea sprung to mind: Perhaps he should contact Harrison's finance Susan; surely she'd be interested in knowing everything about her future husband.

On 8 May, nearly nine weeks after arriving in Bangkok, he and May checked into the Plaza Hotel in downtown Manhattan. The room was only booked for one week. His first priority was to buy her an engagement ring; after that, the next few days consisted of sightseeing, dining out, and drinking heavily. May's favourite bar was Hudson's Dive on Spring Street in Soho. The wife of the owner, Hom Hudson, was originally from a town near where May was raised in Thailand. May worshiped her; she was everything May wanted to be and more. Now in her late thirties, she was still stunningly beautiful and now a successful fashion designer. Hom would often say to her, "Darling, I want to photograph you wearing my clothes." However, it was clear to everybody except naive May that Hom would love to see her without any clothes.

On a few occasions, Daniel suspected that perhaps May enjoyed the occasional sexual encounter with other women. May would flirt outrageously with Hom. More still when an attractive man would pay then admiring glances as they sat together and chatted. May was still grieving Phaung's death, and Daniel enjoyed seeing her happy again. He'd stand back and chat with other drinkers, watching from afar as she drank heavily and flirted with Hom and other men.

Three days into their stay, they were having afternoon drinks at Hudson's. Daniel picked up the courage to contact Susan. Still being a friend of Harrison on Facebook, he sent her a message along with a photograph taken of himself in Koi Samui with Harrison:

"Hello Susan, I have serious information regarding Harrison. Information I'm sure you'll be interested in. Please keep this secret between you and I.

Please, can I trust you?"

When the message was sent, he realised what a fool he'd been. Of course she'd tell her future husband about this message, but it was a start. If anything, Harrison would now know he's in New York and seeking revenge. After finishing his cigarette outside, he made his way into back Hudson's to rescue May from Hom's delicate wandering hands.

Hom and May were both flirting with an attractive bearded man in his forties sitting at their table; he was very smartly dressed. He looked like he worked on Wall Street. They were both extremely taken with him, May especially; she was playing with her hair, something she did when she was flirting. As Daniel approached the table, he noticed the man resembled Harrison; like Bardo, at the resort in Koi Samui, he was an older than him. He feared his mind was playing tricks on him again.

The man stood up to introduce himself; he had a southern American accent and stood over six feet tall. He said, "My name is Richard; pleased to meet y'all, Daniel."

May looked puzzled as Richard introduced himself; she couldn't remember telling him Daniel's name. She giggled to herself, blaming the amount martinis she had. Hom put her arm around her, pulling her uncomfortably closer towards her body, asking if she'd like a coffee. Daniel felt slightly intimidated by this towering, handsome stranger, as he leered at him with piercing dark eyes. He was almost transfixed by him. Richard was certainly intrigued to meet him. Daniel couldn't escape the eye contact; it was clear that Richard was interested in him and not May, as Daniel first thought. After a brief chat with Hom, Richard disappeared into another room to talk privately with Hom's husband, Frank. Daniel knew immediately what business they were discussing. He'd already guessed Frank and Hom were cocaine users and assumed Richard was their dealer.

After a few coffees, May began to liven herself up again. Daniel ordered two bottles of Champagne to be brought to the table, in the hope that Richard would join them, so he could discreetly make a purchase of his own. He didn't want him to know he was an occasional coke user, for fear of telling May. Richard kept his distance after his meeting with Frank; he socialised and mingled with other customers but was forever monitoring Daniel with eye contact. When Richard went to use the washroom, Daniel followed, seeing this as a good opportunity to speak to him in private.

When he entered the washroom, Richard was standing in a cubicle, holding the door open, like he'd been expecting him to follow. There were two lines already chopped up on the closed toilet seat. Richard shut the door behind him as Daniel began to kneel on the floor.

Richard began to rub and massage the back of shoulders, telling him, "You enjoy yourself, boy."

After Daniel took the first line, he stood back, facing Richard, with an uncontrollable desire to kiss him.

He moved forward until his lips were nearly touching Richard's; Richard slowly shook his head and held his shoulders to gently push him away. Daniel felt embarrassed and rejected as Richard took out a small bag of coke and his mobile number. He handed them to him and insisted he call him for more. Daniel took out his wallet, only for Richard to insist, "This sample is for free."

He then passed him his own mobile number as he opened the door, ashamed of his advances.

After a sleepless night at the hotel, the next morning, Daniel lay awake, worrying that his proposal to May might have been in haste. He turned to May, who was also lying awake. Perhaps she was thinking the same. While May took a shower, he checked emails and messages on his phone; to his surprise, Susan had replied to his message:

"Hello Daniel, Harrison has mentioned your name. I'm aware you know him. Yes, I would be interested in information on him. Yes, you can trust me."

Daniel quickly replied:

"Can we meet at Barney's Coffee Shop near the main entrance to Messier Global Shipping? I know you work there; can we meet at 12 today?"

Susan replied:

"I no longer work for Harrison's father, but yes, I will meet you there."

Daniel and May had breakfast at a local patisserie; he apologised, lying that he needed to work today, viewing apartments in Jersey City. After his meeting with Susan, he planned to get high, and May was more than happy to spend the day shopping with Hom.

At 11.45, he waited nervously for Susan at Barney's Coffee Shop, unsure as to exactly what he should tell her. As he sipped his latte, he monitored each person walking through the doors, fearing this could be a setup. As much as he feared Harrison walking in, the thought of seeing him again still excited him. It was exactly noon when she arrived; she recognised him immediately from photographs on Harrison's trip to Thailand.

He stood up to welcome her; his first impression of her was she was pretty and headstrong.

They sat facing each other, both victims, both unsure where to start the conversation.

"I'm no longer with Harrison," she began. "We've been apart for some time now. What you've read in the press is untrue. Billy has friends in the press; they write what he tells them to. They fear him, and he pays them well. Harrison mentioned your name when he was out of it; he said he hurt you. How did he hurt you?"

Daniel felt uncomfortable, not ready to discuss what had happened. He tried to change the subject by offering her coffee.

"Well, Daniel, I'm waiting," she said, declining a drink. "It was you that brought me here. Are you going to tell me what you want?"

"Okay! I'll begin … On his last night at the resort in Koi Samui, Harrison spiked my drink with Xanax; it's used as a date rape drug. He followed me back to my hut, and as the drug kicked in, I lay motionless, unable to move my limbs or scream for help. I asked him if I was going die. 'Probably,' he said, 'after I've given you something to remember me by.' He sodomised me, he violated my body, he raped me! Parker convinced me not to go to the police; we'd taken drugs together days leading up to this. I was scared. I didn't know he was working for his father at that time."

Susan put her hands over her face and began to cry; she looked so saddened but not surprised. Daniel moved from his seat to comfort her; he apologised for upsetting her.

"Why you?" she asked. "Why did he choose you? Why not Ryan or Lucas or anybody else that was there at the time? I'm trying to understand; did he do this as out of hatred towards you, or did he do it because he wanted you? Were you and him having a relationship? I'm sorry. I shouldn't have said that; I'm just trying to understand!"

Daniel couldn't answer this; he shook his head, with his hands over his face. As he did so, Susan noticed the watch he was wearing.

"A Tag Heuer watch, very nice! It's strangely similar to mine. Harrison bought me one after he beat me. I assume he hurt you before he raped you. Say, Daniel, you wanna go for a proper drink?"

Daniel suggested Hudson's. He knew what May would think if she heard he was out drinking with another girl. Drinking at Hudson's together meant he had nothing to hide. He warned Susan that if May should call in there, their story was that she was the girlfriend of one of his friends. At the bar, Daniel found a table and ordered a bottle of Chardonnay as Susan went disappeared to the washroom. When she returned, Daniel couldn't help notice how fast she was talking. She was hyper; he suspected she'd taken cocaine.

"So Daniel, what are you going to do now?"

"Report it to the authorities! He's not going to get away with it."

"Bad idea," she replied. "His father has the best lawyers in the country, if not the world; you wouldn't stand a chance. And besides, if this gets out to the press, it'll destroy his mother. She's a good woman. I can fix up a meeting for you with his father; you just tell him what you've told me. If you threaten to go public with this, he'll listen! When Harrison came back from Thailand, his head was in a bad place. He trashed his father's Brooklyn townhouse. He'd taken crystal that day and was out of control. He was a danger to himself and to me, as I later found out. He had a gun; he was threatening to shoot himself. When I stepped in to help him, he beat me to a pulp. Parker wouldn't take me to hospital; instead, I was treated at home for my injuries by the Fisher's doctor. Billy paid me not to report the incident. Which reminds me, did he tell you about his nanny?"

"Yes, I felt for him," Daniel said. "I can't believe that could have happened to such a wealthy family."

"Do you know the whole story about the nanny?"

"No, just that she'd abused him and they got rid of her."

By this time, they'd polished of a full bottle of wine between them. Daniel went to order another whilst on the way to the washroom for some socialising stimulants. When he returned, Susan was desperate to share a story with him.

"Harrison's nanny was called Maria del Carmen Perez. She was originally from Mexico and moved to America by marrying a Texan guy called Isaac. She had twin boys with him, Roberto and Carlos. She was living a happy life until one day Isaac decided to kill himself, along with their two sons. He'd found out Maria had been cheating on him. Whilst Maria was out shopping for groceries, Isaac locked himself along with the boys in his truck. He'd rigged the truck up with a hose running from the exhaust pipe in through the window. He'd gathered, in his disturbed mental state, that he'd take longer to die and didn't want to witness his five-year-old boys suffer, so he took a shotgun to his mouth and blew his brains out.

"When Maria returned, the neighbours had managed to pull both boys from the truck, only Roberto didn't make it; it was only Carlos who survived. Carlos was taken into care and later adopted. Maria couldn't cope with him; she lost her mind and had a serious breakdown. She moved to New York and got a job as a maid for the Fishers at their mansion in Westhampton. She eventually became Harrison's nanny. She'd been stable whilst working as a maid, but when left in charge of Harrison, it brought back memories of her loss; she never got over the loss her family, which is probably why she treated Harrison so badly."

Susan disappeared yet again to the washroom to powder her nose, whilst Daniel called May to let her know where he was, telling her who he'd met up with. Still out shopping with Hom, she said she'd join them later. When Susan returned, she continued with the story.

"Well, here's where this story becomes interesting: It's said that the Fishers had her deported her back to Mexico on criminal grounds, but I doubt that's true. Her son Carlos came to New York in search of her when he was eighteen; they had a reconciliation. This was when Eva first started seeing Billy; she took pity on Carlos and helped set him up with a job and somewhere to live here in Manhattan, so he could be close to his mum, and that's how Maria repaid her generosity: by abusing her son! I heard that when he knew she'd disappeared without a trace, Carlos started blackmailing the Fishers. I also heard that Harrison befriended Carlos when he was fifteen and still has contact with him."

"Yes, I overheard him speak to Carlos in Thailand."

Susan laughed and looked around the room to check nobody was listening.

"There are many rumours regarding Carlos; nobody has seen him since his mother disappeared. People have said that Carlos is a figment of Harrison's imagination, you know, like an imaginary friend; spooky or what? It's even been said that it was Harrison himself who was behind blackmailing his own father. Others say that he does exist and that he's Harrison's secret gay lover; how sick is that? Sleeping with the son of the woman who abused him. I know Harrison has fooled around with other guys; that wouldn't surprise me."

May and Hom walked into the bar, staring at Daniel and Susan with disconcerting expressions. Frank had called Hom previously, telling her Daniel and a girl were drinking heavily and getting high together in the bar. As they made their way to the table, Susan got up to leave; she stumbled to her feet and struggled to walk in a straight line. Daniel escorted her out onto the sidewalk to call her a cab. She put her arms around him and wished him luck with Billy, and then she kissed him, thanking him for the drinks. As he waved her off in the cab, May watched from the window, arms crossed. She wasn't happy.

At nine o'lock, Daniel woke on top of their hotel bed after passing out earlier. May was sitting at the dresser, adding the finishing touches to her make-up. She completely ignored him as she went for the door.

"May, May, where are you going?"

"I'm meeting Hom; don't wait up."

"Wait for me. I'll join you."

"I don't want you anywhere near me! You were high on coke today with that girl. You know my feelings towards drugs."

"Just wait a minute; your new girlfriend's continuously high on coke. You didn't give her a hard time about it."

"I'm not in a relationship with her, and she doesn't lie to me."

"Not yet; are you in a relationship with her? If she has her way, you'll be sleeping with her soon."

May slammed the door behind her. Daniel continued to lay on the bed with his hands over his face, trying to get his thoughts together. After an hour, he showered, got dressed, and made his way to Hudson's to make peace with her. Before entering the bar, he lit a cigarette on the sidewalk and looked inside. May was not with Hom tonight; she was sitting at a table, talking intimately to Richard. He didn't go in. He couldn't justify to himself marching in and asking questions, not after he'd made a pass at this man.

The next morning, May ordered breakfast to be brought to the room. She was in a happier mood today. He'd received a message from Susan:

> "Billy Fisher will see you today at 11.30 at Messier Global
> Shipping building. Be on time and dress smartly. There
> is a heart in the man somewhere. However, he might try
> to twist things. Just remember: You're the victim. I'm off
> to Europe tomorrow to do some travelling.
> Best of luck.
>
> Susan. Xxx

He told May that he had an important meeting today that could earn Hugo's development company an incredible profit; he thought, *She'll be mad about leaving her again.* Instead, she was more than happy for him to go; she'd made prior arrangements to visit Hom at her studio. As he kissed her goodbye, something had changed between them. The kiss was nothing more than a routine, not the usual meaningful gesture of affection. As he left the hotel, he feared that they were drifting apart.

He arrived at the Messier Building in midtown Manhattan at 11.10; at exactly 11.20, one of Billy's personal security guards came to collect him. Billy's office was on the fortieth floor of the building; in the elevator, he felt uncomfortable as he nervously tried to make conversation with the security guard. Apart from the occasional yes and no, he was determined not to exchange any pleasantries with the visitor.

The elevator door opened to reveal a large double door with a plaque that read "William Frazier Fisher, MD." His heart began to pound with fear. He reminded himself that there was no turning back now; this was his moment. This was where he could get the upper hand; this was where he'd get justice.

Billy's office was huge; he wasn't there when he was shown in. The security guard left him alone, telling him, "Please take a seat. Mr Fisher, Billy, will be with you shortly."

Instead of sitting, he roamed around the office until he spotted pictures of his family. There was a glamorous picture of Eva in a modelling shot, another one of Eva holding her youngest sons, all five when they were babies, and one of Harrison looking fresh faced, standing outside Harvard University; he looked so young and innocent. As he stared at the picture, he heard a door close, and a voice spoke from behind him:

"We had high hopes for him back then; we were proud of him. He could have gone on to do great things with his life."

Daniel jumped with fear as Billy brushed past him, lifted the picture from off the desk, and looked at it with great sadness. After placing the picture down, he introduced himself. Billy wasn't as tall as he'd imagined. He was friendly and not as intimidating as he'd feared.

"Susan tells me you're here to talk about Harrison. I believe you know my son?"

"Yes sir; however, I think you know why I'm here."

"*Let's cut to the chase, son. It's been over a month since Harrison's vacation in Thailand; why now? Why has it taken you this long to see me?*"

"*Because I've been comforting and supporting my girlfriend over the loss of her mother. Her name was Phaung; she recently lost her battle with cancer. The same woman who Parker threatened; she knew what your son had done to me but was too scared to speak on out it.*"

"*Tell me, why didn't you report this alleged assault?*"

"*You have Parker to thank for that; he was the one who manipulated me into not reporting it.*"

"*Parker tells me you were having …, shall we say, a homosexual relationship with my son. In fact, he followed you and Harrison back to your hut when this alleged assault happened. He thought to leave you both alone, alone to do whatever you people do in private.*"

"*That's not true; we were close friends. Parker was nowhere to be seen later that night; he was with a girl called Sai Meesanang, who works at the resort. Feel free to ask her; whilst you're asking for proof, please feel free to ask the doctor who treated me the next day. I had Xanax in my blood; Harrison spiked my drink. I was barely conscious when he sodomised me. The same doctor also found internal bleeding from my anus. It's obviously doctor–patient confidentiality, but if the police were involved, I'm sure they'd be given that information.*"

"*I've heard enough of this; you don't have actual evidence. Nobody but you and my son knows what really happened in hut that night.*"

"*Your absolutely right, sir. Thank you for meeting me. I see I'm wasting my time here. I shall now report this to the relevant authorities. By the way, Mr Fisher, I still feel sympathy for Harrison. Like I said, we were close friends. We shared secrets; he told me secrets about his family and his nanny, Maria Perez.*"

As Daniel headed for the door, Billy stepped hastily in front of him to keep him from leaving. Gone was the charming man who'd welcomed him in earlier; now stood an angry, calculating businessman, desperate to strike a deal.

"*So, Daniel, is this blackmail? Are you here for money?*"

"No, I don't need your money. I want justice for what your son has put me through. I want him to suffer! And I want Parker to suffer for threatening a dying lady. Mr Fisher, you can't expect me to just walk away from this and to keep quiet, can you?"

He told Daniel to take a seat and asked one of his secretaries to bring in some coffee, and then disappeared into the same door where he entered. As the minutes passed by, Daniel feared he'd reappear with either Harrison or Parker to contradict his story. After twenty-five minutes, he entered again, followed by a man clutching a laptop. Billy took Daniel to one side as the man set the laptop on a desk.

"I'm prepared to make a deal with you. I don't want my family's name dragged through the dirt. You say you don't want money? I don't believe you; money talks, and money silences. I'm willing to pay you $1 million. But Daniel, this comes with terms and conditions.

"On receipt of this money, you will sign this contract I've just had drawn up, which will legally forbid you from ever speaking about my family. I assure you that Harrison will be dealt with accordingly, and you will forget ever meeting him. I also insist you leave New York as soon as possible. It would be in your best interest to follow these rules; now, do I make myself clear?"

After signing the contract, Daniel was led over to the man with the laptop to have the money deposited electronically into his account. The same security guard entered the room to escort him out of the building. Without a handshake or goodbye, Billy made a call on his mobile and disappeared into the next room. The call was made to Harrison, who, unaware to him, was sitting here in the main reception area of the Messier Building.

Harrison didn't answer his call, he knew who was in the building with his father and wasn't interested in the outcome. He didn't care what punishment was about to come his way. The only thing that mattered now was being this close to Daniel. Ever since he'd arrived in New York, Harrison has been monitoring his every move, waiting for this day to come. The elevator door opened, and Harrison held a newspaper up against his face. He discreetly

watched with admiration as Daniel walked past him with his head held high,
sporting an enthusiastic smile.

It wasn't until he left the building and stood on the sidewalk in the pouring
rain that the amount of money sunk in. He stared up at the dark clouds,
with the rain beating down on his face, as people clutching umbrellas and
newspapers over their heads forced their way past him to avoid the downpour.

"Yes, yes," he said to himself, as swept back his wet hair with both hands; the
rain pelted down on his face, almost cleansing his soul. He felt the overwhelming
relief of closure and euphoria of yet more wealth sending him into an all-time
high. Completely unaware of his surroundings, Harrison discreetly followed
as he headed for shelter under a neighbouring building's doorway canopy to
light a cigarette and call May. As he waited for her to answer, he quickly put
a story together as to why he had something to celebrate, the story being he'd
struck upon a mega deal that would make himself and uncle Hugo a fortune.
When she answered, she sounded upset; when asked why, she said she'd explain
later at the hotel. For now, realising he had a few hours to kill and the fact he
needed to leave New York as soon as possible, he called Richard to buy cocaine
from him for his trip.

Richard, who was busy at his apartment, gave him his address and
suggested he get a cab over to see him; his apartment was on Eleventh Avenue
East, a ten-minute cab ride from Messier Building.

Daniel was taken by surprise when he answered the door; he was wearing
nothing more than loose sweat pants and a vest, hardly recognisable out of his
smart suit. He was busy packing for his return to Florida the next morning.
Daniel couldn't help but look at his muscular physique and his heavily tattooed
left arm; for a man in his forties, he looked extremely fit.

He sat him on the sofa and cracked open two beers; when offered a line,
he firmly declined, fearing he'd make a pass at him again. Instead, he asked
him what he and May were discussing last night. Richard's answer was that
it was Hom's idea; not knowing he was gay, she tried to set them up together.
She'd taken an instant dislike to Daniel and thought May could do better

for herself with a more mature man. Richard told May he was gay, and they joked about how manipulating Hom could be. He also told Daniel that he liked May; however, he asked if he was sure she was what he really wanted.

Daniel was furious with this intervening in his relationship and snapped, "This is none of your business."

"Well, boy, that's my intervening done between you and your girl. I'm through with being used," Richard said, suddenly realising he'd said too much and changing the subject before Daniel could ask any more questions.

Richard got up and went to a drawer; he took out an eight ball of coke and threw it into Daniel's lap, saying, "I need to get on with my packing, boy. I'll give you this for your trip, free of charge. You call me if you need any more; I'll have a courier at your door wherever you are in the U.S. You look me up if you're ever in Florida, or call me if you ever need to talk. I'll be there for you. You take care now."

Daniel was shown to the door, confused by his generosity but also grateful. As he said goodbye, he shook his hand and looked deeply into his eyes. Still holding his hand, he said, "You'd better be sure what you really want with your girlfriend; make your decision and stick to it, you hear me?"

CHAPTER 8

Tough Love

After he left Richard's apartment, with Harrison still following, he called in at Premier Autos, a used car dealer near upper Eleventh Avenue. Before being paid off by Billy, he'd planned to buy a big old Jeep or GMC 4x4 vehicle to see them through their road trip. But after his million-dollar payout, he wanted something far more extravagant. That car was a nearly new 4x4 Porsche Cayenne Turbo S. He'd seen it earlier parked outside the dealer's on the way to Richard's and knew immediately he wanted it. As he the dealer showed him the interior features, Harrison watched from the back of his waiting cab.

At first, he wanted to jump out and approach him, meet him face to face and beg forgiveness, imagining he'd accept his apology for what he did to him. In his mind, he was convinced Daniel was not here to seek revenge and certainly not closure. He was here in New York City to be close to him and so he could hunt him down like prey. Not to be shot dead, but to be kept for eternity, as a companion and lover. As he went for the door handle, something stopped him; the timing wasn't right. Not here, not like this, and certainly not whilst May was still on the scene, for whilst she was still with him, he would continue to fool himself that he was in love with her. But the time would come, soon, when he would have him all to himself.

Harrison's only ever had Carlos as a close companion; after Maria was sent away, Carlos would visit him secretly. He was his first crush, his first wet dream, the person he fantasised having sex with when he first started masturbating. Carlos encouraged him to smoke cigarettes at thirteen and then pot at fifteen. Carlos also introduced him to cocaine at seventeen. It was at the age of seventeen, when they were both high, Harrison made a pass at him. Carlos was repulsed by his advances and pushed him away, furious. He disappeared after that; he was gone from his life for nearly two years but came back eventually, only to remain close friends.

Harrison instructed the cab driver to pull away; instead of a confrontation, he sent Daniel a text message: "You finally got the car; it suits you."

Daniel inquisitively reached for his phone; his eyes lit up with delight when he saw who the message was from. He discreetly looked around the auto lot, trying not to grin with excitement at the thought that Harrison had finally caught up with him. Without any haggling over the $89,000 sales price, he bought the Porsche using Hugo's Tampa address for documentation and told the salesman to have it ready for collection tomorrow morning.

When he arrived back at the hotel, May was in tears; as he walked through the door, she ran to him with open arms, apologising for her behaviour over the past few days. She'd had a terrible day with Hom; when she arrived at her studio, she was told to wait whilst Hom was having an important meeting. She waited for an hour before Hom would see her. The important meeting was nothing more than she and her French photographer Thiery and a young model downing two bottles of Champagne whilst disgussing a photo shoot. Hom was also clearly high; she was obnoxious. For some reason, she'd misread May's intention for being her friend. She believed May was nothing more than a wannabe model, desperately looking for work. She threw a selection of dresses at her, insisting she change into one now and look pretty for the camera; then, she might consider employing her.

May overheard her having a private conversation with Thiery, in French, she explained to him, "May's very pretty yet somewhat dumb.

She hasn't a dime to her name; she's also naive, gullible, and desperate for work. Flatter her on her looks, and I'm sure she'll do anything you want her to do."

Hom didn't realise May spoke fluent French; she then joined in on the conversation, telling Hom in French, "Go fuck yourself, you deluded, ageing, manipulating, talentless bitch. Perhaps you should stick to speaking Siamese and English; your French is poor, almost unrecognizable. I'll be off now; I've got an interview. Sorry, I forgot to tell you I want to teach language here at one of America's better universities."

May couldn't have been more happy when Daniel told her they were leaving New York in the morning. As he wiped away tears in her eyes, it filled his heart with joy that once again he'd made her happy. At that moment in time, as he kissed her and her face turned to joy, there was nobody on this earth he'd rather be with. He also had another surprise for her: He insisted he make a payment into her bank account, to the sum of $50,000, justifying this by the promise he made to Phaung – that he would always love her and make her financially secure. The money was also for their road trip, giving her independence; if an emergency should occur, she'd always have access to money. They didn't go out that night; instead, they ordered room service and joyfully lazed on the bed, eating, drinking wine, and planning a route for the road trip adventure commencing tomorrow.

In North Fork, Long Island, Eva Fisher was watching the security monitor with suspicion as Harrison's black Range Rover Sport made its way through the beach house's electric gate. She instinctively knew something was wrong; unexpected visits from him meant he was in trouble. Even at the age of twenty-five, he'd always come running to his mother for help. Just as he entered the house, Eva took a phone call from Billy; she made her way out onto the deck, instructing Harrison to watch his younger brothers in the family room. That room opened up out onto the deck, which stood directly on the beach. With the landline telephone pushed against her ear, she looked at Harrison in disgust whilst wiping a tear from her eye. From just one look, he knew his worst fears had just came true. He knew what that phone call was about and he knew what Billy was telling her.

Earlier today, after seeing Daniel at the auto dealer, he didn't go to see Billy. Instead, he returned to the Brooklyn apartment, only to find the locks had been changed and all his belongings had been left in the janitor's office. He also knew that Daniel had been to see his father, looking at expense cars. It was obvious Billy had paid him off.

Eve finished the phone call and lit a cigarette; he knew she only smoked when deeply upset. He walked out onto the deck and on to the beach, to where she now stood, looking out to sea.

"Mom, Mom! I can explain. Please look at me."

Eve turned to him with a look of disgust; without warning, she struck him over the head with the telephone. He dropped, knees first, onto to the sand, with his hands over his face, like a cowering dog.

"I've raised a monster," she said. "I've brought a monster into this world who's capable of beating a woman and doing that despicable thing to that boy in Thailand. You disgust me! I wished I hadn't had you. I wished to God I'd had you aborted."

Both distraught from what they just saw from the deck, Mason and Giles started to scream and cry; as Eva walked over to them, she turned to Harrison once again.

"He's disinherited you, you know; he's cut you off without a cent. As we speak, his security team is on their way over here to remove you. He's forbidden you from having any contact with your brothers; he thinks you're a threat to them."

"What about you, Mom? Am I forbidden to see you?"

"I can't help you now. I want you to go. I want you to leave now, right now. I don't want your brothers to see you removed from your home."

She wouldn't allow him to say goodbye to them, for fear it might upset the boys further. She waked him to his car; as he got behind the wheel, she took out a credit card.

"Here, take this; you've got your car, and you've got money. Baby, it's the drugs that turn you into a monster, it's not you. Please, please try to stay off the drugs, I beg you. Make peace with the people you've hurt, and make me proud. I love you, baby, take care."

Harrison drove off, leaving Eva with her hand over her mouth in tears. He drove aimlessly for an hour, unsure where to go or who to turn to. He tried phoning several people but nobody answered his calls, as if everybody in his circle of friends had deserted him now, knowing he was broke and disowned by his family. Halfway between North Fork and the city, he pulled off the highway in Queens and parked alongside Meadow Lake to think. There, he sat in his car in tears; distraught, he reached into his glove box for his gun, contemplating taking his own life.

It was 1.30 a.m. Daniel lay awake, thinking about today's events, about the money and the message from Harrison. As the feelings of hate and anger for him were subsiding, his feelings of affection and lust grew more dominant. He felt satisfied now that justice had been done; his mind was finally at peace. He reached for his phone to study the message again, searching for a hidden meaning; inside, he was tormented with the urge to reply. He knew he would, at some point, and without thinking too much, he typed a simple "Thank you" as a peace offering. As he switched off the phone, he knew that now was the time to focus purely on May, although deep inside, he knew this would be difficult.

Harrison's right hand trembled with fear as he reached for the gun in his lap; his tearful eyes closed as he aimed the gun to his mouth. As the gun balanced on his bottom lip and his finger put pressure on the trigger, as if by fate, he heard a text message alert. He laughed uncontrollably when he saw who it was from. Shaking his head and smiling, he gently rubbed the screen with his thumb over Daniel's simple message, thinking, "He must be my destiny; my one and only has saved me."

The next morning, May looked in horror at the car Daniel had bought. When he told her he'd bought a Porsche, she assumed it to be an old classic convertible that he'd simply dispose of at the end of the road trip. At first, she was saddened by his choice of car; she had a romantic image of her driving for days with the warm desert wind blowing through her hair, holding hands with the man she loved. She was scared to ask how much he'd paid for it; she knew it was ridiculously expensive. When she climbed inside, she was overcome by the prestigious new-car smell. After she luxuriated in the sumptuous red-leather interior and played with the touchscreen communication management system, with features such as sat-nav, Internet, and even TV, her opinion of the car completely changed.

After leaving New York, their first stop was lunch at a roadside diner in Harrisburg, Pennsylvania. They were both tired and planned to stop for the day after another two hours. May was keen to get into the driver's seat of the Porsche and insisted Daniel have beer with his food. Unknown to her, he was also knocking back shots of whisky whenever she used the washroom; this gave him an appetite for a little cocaine to round off his meal. He thought better of it in the washroom and stared in the mirror, almost hearing himself say, "No, now is the time to change." He took the eight ball of coke out of his pocket and held it over the toilet, contemplating flushing it; suddenly, the fear of being stranded on his trip without it got the better of him, and he put it away, in case of emergency.

After lunch, they asked a lady in the parking lot to take a photo of them for Daniel's Facebook. The photo was of him holding May with his arms wrapped around her, leaning back on him against the car. May smiled at the camera as Daniel kissed her neck, also staring at the camera, to show how happy and deeply in love they were. May believed this to be another attempt by Daniel to make his ex-girlfriend Emma jealous, but unknown to her, there was somebody else he wanted this to make envious.

Their planned route was a 2,500-mile drive west to Las Vegas, where they planned to get married. After that, they'd spend their honeymoon split into two destinations: San Francisco and Los Angeles. Daniel wanted the wedding to be just the two of them, but May, who was desperate to meet his family, was now pressuring him to fly his mother and Uncle Hugo over. He'd hoped by then he'd have plucked up the courage to tell her truth about his nonexistent job for his uncle. He'd already worked out a story to tell her; the truth was that he wanted to impress her by having a successful career and the money he was now extravagantly spending was from his inheritance. After California, they wanted to visit the Grand Canyon before heading south to Mexico, and then east, visiting Dallas and New Orleans en route to Florida, where they'd originally planned to meet up with his mum, who'd planned a holiday staying at Hugo's villa.

May loved driving, especially driving the Porsche; she'd compiled herself a playlist of nearly two hundred songs to play when it was her time to drive. She'd enjoyed herself that much she'd covered two hundred miles whilst Daniel slept in the passenger seat. He didn't wake up until she stopped at a fuelling station in New Stanton, about sixty minutes from Pittsburgh. She wanted him to book a nearby hotel whilst she filled the tank. Instead, he booked a room in the five-star Omni William Penn Hotel in Pittsburgh.

Daniel thought she'd be pleased to be staying at such a grand hotel. She was far from happy when she found out how far away it was. In fact, she was furious. She was tired after hours behind the wheel and didn't fancy driving another hour into Pittsburgh. She just wanted a roadside motel not far from where they were getting gas. She soon had a change of heart when they arrived at the hotel. As she stood in the lobby, she was speechless. It was breathtakingly beautiful, the ultimate in luxury, a classic hotel with a history. It had played host to movie stars, politicians, and heads of state.

After they settled into their room that evening, Daniel opened a bottle of wine and ran the extra-large bath for them to luxuriate in before dinner. He quickly stopped the taps to the sound of May screaming ecstatically. She'd just received an email from her father Thomas. He'd not been in touch with over four months, and she was beginning to fear that he'd not wanted anymore contact with her. Thomas had recently moved house and mislaid her email address. His old computer had broken, and he never received any of Phaung's reply letters. But when Sirichai wrote to him with concerns over the deeds of the house, he realised she'd died.

May was overjoyed with this news. In fact, Thomas now wanted to video call her. Daniel wasn't convinced by his sudden urge to reconcile with his daughter and wondered if perhaps he was more interested in her property. Not wanting to upset May, Daniel kept his theory to himself.

Over dinner, she talked endlessly about her father; in fact, she talked about nothing else. Daniel was getting bored and wondered that maybe she'd rather be in the UK being reacquainted than being here in the United States. The more he tried to change the subject back to their road trip, the more she reverted the conversation back to him. She hardly touched her food and only took one sip of wine. Her mind was clearly somewhere else. He insisted she go back to the room alone to either call or video call him whilst he had a few drinks in the bar.

The bar was full to capacity with the aftermath of an undertakers' convention, all abusing their company's generosity by consuming as much alcohol as possible. He wasn't short of anybody to talk to; he was very popular with the conventioneers, all bored with endless business talk. To them, he was a breath of fresh air. He loved the attention and enjoyed meeting new people from various states, especially Clara, a lesbian who kept his glass topped up with tequila. From southern Texas, she had a no-nonsense approach to life and kept him in hysterical laughter with her dark sense of humour.

It was nearly two o'clock when he decided to call it a night; they exchanged numbers and he happily staggered away in search of his room after a fun-filled, drunken night. He couldn't remember a night he'd had more fun and felt so relaxed; he worried that this, the first night of their road trip, that he enjoyed the company of a stranger more than his time together with his fiancée.

When he finally found his room, he'd expected May to be furious with him for being out so late. Instead, she asked him if he'd enjoyed his night and apologised for not joining him at the bar. She even helped him undress after he fell to floor whilst trying to remove his trousers; surprisingly, she laughed and found it amusing that he was so drunk.

He woke up the next morning, feeling sick and overwhelmed with guilt that he had had such a good night without May. That was, until she woke him. It was seven o'clock, and she was eager to press on and hit the road early. She demanded he get dressed and join her for breakfast. Feeling rough and still drunk from last night, this was the last thing he wanted. He came up with a plan to stay another night and tried to sell that idea by tempting her with a morning at the hotel spa and a visit to the Andy Warhol Museum (he knew she liked him). But to his surprise, she wasn't having any of it. She was adamant that they should leave as early as possible. Thinking this to be unreasonable, he argued his point that there was no rush: He was rich, they were young, they had all the time in the world.

This started their first full-blown heated argument; it was Daniel who eventually backed down. He agreed to leave early on the condition that she drive again; however, this didn't come as a hardship for her. After all, she enjoyed driving; it gave her a feeling of being in control.

The second morning of their road trip was far from a pleasant experience; it was pouring with rain, and they hardly said a word to each other. Daniel was also sick from last night's overindulgence, and May, who was already unhappy with driving in the heavy rain, had to occasionally pull over to allow him to throw up at the roadside. Although she'd never admit it to him, she was beginning to wish she listened to him and stayed another night at the hotel. In between bouts of sickness, he was sitting comfortably in passenger seat with a smug expression on his face.

May was getting annoyed and feeling left out by his outbreaks of laughter from exchanging text messages with Clara. After pulling over for the third time for him to be sick, she grew furious with his endless text messaging banter. May reached for his phone to see who he'd been messaging. Just at the moment of holding his phone, he received another message.

This time, the text was from Harrison; it said simply, "We should be together."

She looked puzzled, the name was vaguely familiar to her.

As Daniel wiped his mouth with a wet wipe and headed back to the car, she quickly placed the phone back. At that moment, she remembered where she'd heard the name Harrison. After driving away again, she waited calmly and suspiciously to see his reaction when he read the message. When he did, a look of horror covered his face, and he immediately begged her to pull over to be sick again. Only this time, he dropped to his knees in the wet grass; in agony, he clutched his stomach and sobbed like a baby, heaving with nothing more inside him to throw up except for painful stomach acid. When he climbed back into the car, he looked distressed. It was at that moment she knew the message was troubling him, was far more painful than the vomiting.

He slept after that and didn't wake until she pulled up at a diner in Richmond, Indiana.

"We need to talk," May said as she released her seat belt.

They took a table next to the window and both stared out at the rain pelting down.

"You go first, Daniel. You've been so distant today, and it's not just because of your hangover. Something's bothering you. I need to know what it is. We can't go on like this."

"You want me to tell you? Then I'll tell you: Leaving early this morning, I feel as you want to hurry our time here together. As I said, there no rush. Is it because of your father? Would you rather be with him? Am I not enough?"

A tear formed in her eye as she stared out of the window again.

"You didn't ask me how it went with my father, Daniel."

"I'm sorry."

"It's okay; it's not important, and he's not important. I want to leave early because I cried in that room last night. I cried all alone whilst you were getting drunk in the bar. I found out last night that my father has been living in Thailand with his new wife, Daniel. He's been living in Pattaya for six months, 150 kilometres away from my university in Bangkok."

She broke down into tears, and Daniel moved around the table to comfort her.

"Why didn't he come and find me? It hurts so much that he was so close and never bothered to contact me. He could have come to my mother's funeral. Also, he asked about the condition of the house; he wants to sell it, Daniel. Sirichai will be homeless!"

He held her in his arms and wiped away the tears, seeing how devastated she was, he quickly thought of a solution. He asked her to call her father again tonight. "Well, here's what you do," he explained. "You tell him the house is in need of serious repair, and you offer him a small amount to purchase it from him, okay? If he agrees, then you use the money I gave you to buy it. Now, can we order some food? I'm starving."

She smiled, kissed him, and thanked him from her heart; she'd planned to ask him who Harrison was, but, under the circumstances, this didn't feel the right time. After lunch, Daniel took the keys from her, insisting it was his turn to drive. As they walked back to the car, the sun came out, and his hangover was now a distant memory. Their next planned stopover was in Indianapolis; it was May's turn to select and book a hotel for the night. Now that the dark cloud of her father was lifted, the drive was filled with joy and anticipation for the fulfilled times ahead.

That joy was short-lived when they pulled up at the Beech Grove Inn parking lot. Daniel looked in horror; the general appearance of the hotel was reminiscent of an American horror film he'd seen. The parking lot was littered with cigarette butts, and weeds were growing up through the asphalt. The other vehicles parked were a selection of monster trucks, contractor vans, and motor bikes.

"No way, we are not staying here," he said, turning his nose up at what looked like the worst motel in America.

"You're a snob, Daniel Reed," she replied. "Come on, it'll be fun. Trust me. It's only for one night. It'll be an experience."

The room was no better, basic, but reasonably clean. Daniel, walked suspiciously around the room and inspected behind each of the pictures hanging on the walls, searching for hidden cameras. May stood back, confused; she looked at him, thinking he'd gone crazy.

"I remember that film now," he said. "A young couple were stranded in a rundown motel and were brutally murdered in their room. Their room was fitted with hidden video cameras to film a snuff video. Are you sure you want to stay here?"

"I'll take my chances," she said. "The only thing that's scaring me is you, you madman!" She walked over to kiss him.

Later, while she took a bath, Daniel stood outside the door, having a cigarette whilst sending text messages to Clara and Richard, jokingly telling them he was staying at the Bates Motel. A souped-up Chrysler pulled up to the next room, and a drug dealer type looked suspiciously around the lot whilst he remained in his car, waiting for his neighbouring guests to come out to him. His neighbours were a young couple; she was attractive but looked like she'd not had a good night's sleep in ten years. Her boyfriend walked around the car, admiring it. She stuck her head through the window to talk to the driver. Daniel noticed him pass her a small package; the girl turned and spotted Daniel looking at them.

He smiled and nodded, as if to let her know "I know what you're doing; enjoy!" After the drop-off was done, she winked at Daniel on the way back to her room. He laughed to himself, thinking this was a hard-core drug deal. Not young partygoers buying speed or cocaine to get off their tits on a Saturday night, not like back home in Manchester. This was full-on shit – crystal-meth, crack, and even heroin being sold to junkies whose lives depended on another hit.

Surprisingly, they spent an enjoyable first night together at the Beech Lodge Inn. May loved the simplicity of just them eating pizza together, lying on the bed and watching TV. That was until they heard the girl next door screaming and moaning in ecstasy. Daniel laughed to himself; he knew these cries of joy were not just the result of a good fuck. These screams of ecstasy were the result of a chemical mood enhancer. Disgusted by the sexual noise pollution, May reached for the TV remote control to turning the volume up as high as possible. The more she became infuriated, the more the screams turned him on. As she made herself comfortable under the duvet, he knew sex was definitely out of the question tonight. He lay back on the bed with his hands behind his head and fantasised about joining them next door.

As his eyes began to close and he began to drift off to sleep, May turned to him and asked, "Who's Harrison?"

The mere suggestion of his name was nauseating, especially being woken with it.

He got out of bed and lit a cigarette, saying, "I met him at the resort; we did a few excursions together. Why do you ask?"

"His name flashed up on your mobile when you were being sick." Worried that she'd read the message, he quickly put a story together. "He asked me to look him up if I was ever in the USA. He's not someone I want to see again; he's not a nice person."

May knew he was lying; she remembered now where she'd heard his name. Suspicious about this mystery friend, she tried to recall what her mother had mentioned about their friendship. She lay wake for hours, worrying, worried why he'd lie to her.

They were woken at 4 a.m. to sound of the Porsche's car alarm; a truck had accidentally reversed into it and driven off without leaving details. The truck had caused extensive damage to the rear bumper. May was mortified; she blamed herself for choosing the hotel, and to make matters worse, the hotel had no CCTV in the parking lot.

As usual, Daniel wouldn't let her take the blame; he reassured her that this could have happened anywhere.

Later that morning, the mechanic repairing the damage told them, depending on parts, it could take up to four days to fix. Not wanting to haul their luggage to another hotel, they decided to keep their room and travel light, staying at another hotel. This was Daniel's turn to choose hotel. After packing for just one night, they set off in a cab to Indy airport. After a one-hour-and-fifteen-minute flight, they landed at Chicago airport, where they were collected by the Langham Hotel limousine service. They were booked into the finest hotel in Chicago, if not in America. May was far from happy; to her, this was an unnecessary extravagance. When she discovered he'd paid $3,000 for one night, she accused him of having no self-control, with little respect for money. He knew she'd be annoyed when he booked it, in fact, he purposely chose this hotel, simply to piss her off. When she was lecturing him about money, he nearly told her, "This isn't half as much as what it'll cost to get the Porsche repaired, thanks to your choice of hotel."

They spent the afternoon shopping and doing a little sightseeing from the back seat of the cab. As much as he insisted on buying her something to wear for dinner, she refused on principle of how much the hotel cost.

She even insisted on having room service instead of eating in one of the hotel's fine restaurants. This was by no means a hardship; the suite was stunning, with its hardwood flooring, floor-to-ceiling windows, and breathtaking views of the Chicago skyline and river. She was secretly overjoyed with their stay at the hotel, far more than she'd admit to; at least she didn't have to listen to the neighbouring junkies having sex at the Beech Grove Inn.

In the cab on return to Beech Grove Lodge the next day, Daniel thought it was time to tell her the truth about Harrison. She'd quizzed him again on the flight back to Indianapolis. He was getting tired of lying to her and believed one day he'd catch up with him. As the cab pulled into the parking lot, he was convinced that day had come. Out of the window, he spotted a black Range Rover Sport, identical to Harrison's. Like a sixth sense, he knew it was him. He'd been expecting him. As May paid for the cab, he stood and stared fearfully at the car.

"You look like you've seen a ghost," May said inquisitively as she went to investigate what he was staring at.

"I wish it were a ghost," he replied. "We need to talk; we need to talk now."

He ushered May into the room, where he sat on the bed, staring into space, not knowing where to start.

"I'll make us coffee," she said, worrying about what he was about to confess.

He declined the coffee; instead, he needed something stronger. He told her he was going out to the nearby drinks store; he needed something to calm his nerves. She watched, confused, as he took to his feet, almost in a trance, and made his way to the door. Outside, he once again stared at the car and looked around the hotel in fear of what his emotions would be if he was to see him again. His phone vibrated from inside his pocket; it was a text message from Harrison: "Room 102."

He walked hesitantly towards the room. As he got closer, he froze as the door slowly opened. There he stood, facing him: Harrison. His looks had changed dramatically; he looked a shadow of his former self. Gone was the muscular physique and fair hair; his hair had grown dark and his face a ghostly white. He looked like he'd not slept in weeks; by his sad expression, he could see he was on a downer.

Daniel shook his head when Harrison asked him to come in; instead, he walked to a recreational area hidden at the rear of the hotel. May had found his wallet in their flight bag. She knew there was something or someone at the hotel of pressing importance that he needed to deal with. Clutching the wallet, she set out to follow him. As she stepped out into the parking lot, she saw Daniel with Harrison following behind. She immediately knew who it was; she recognised him from the magazine photo.

Daniel sat on a bench, staring at the floor, as Harrison took a seat next to him.

"From my heart," Harrison began, "I'm truly sorry for what I did to you. I wanted to punish you for rejecting me; God help me, if I could go back in time. How have you been? You're looking good. America suits you."

"How have I been? I'm better now; the war in my head is at peace. I'm getting better every day. I'm a different person now. I'm not that fucked-up victim you left behind in Samui. What are you doing here, Harrison? How did you know I was here?"

"I'm here to apologise, and I'm here because you and I could still be together."

"Together? May and I, we're in love and to be married."

"I know you don't love her. Stop fooling yourself; look me in the eye and tell me you don't have feelings for me."

At this point, Daniel felt confident. He wanted to hurt him one last time. He wanted him to suffer. A hotel maid slammed a fire exit door behind her whilst she lit a cigarette.

Harrison quickly turned and snapped, "Hey lady, can't you see we're talking?"

As she rushed back in, he could see a reflection of May discreetly watching at the corner of the building.

Daniel turned and to look him in the eye, saying, "You're right. I do have feelings for you, and you're right, I don't love her, but I will learn to love her. She's good for me. You're what I want, but she's what I need. What future would you and I have together? We both take pleasure in hurting each other. One of us will end up dead, if not both of us."

"I'll be checking out soon, Daniel, I'll be outta your life for good. One last thing before I go: let me hold you in my arms. Let's just call it a farewell gift."

They both stood up, and Harrison put his arms around him; the embrace was intense. Daniel stared over his shoulder with sadness, knowing that Harrison was right: He did have feelings for him; he never wanted to let go of him. Harrison turned to where May was watching; she'd seen enough. Harrison smirked at her as she to where the two of them were still holding each other.

"You forgot your wallet, Daniel," May said as they separated, still looking into each other's eyes.

Harrison turned to her and said, "Hey, Thai girl. He chose you; you got your boy. Be happy."

He walked away as May stood staring at Daniel, waiting for him to say something. Speechless, he just watched Harrison walk away.

She could see he was upset; as he sat back down on the bench, she calmly walked back to the room. When he returned ten minutes later, he walked past her, sitting on the bed, and walked into the bathroom. She followed him and looked in disbelief as he took out his cocaine.

"Drugs? Daniel, why? This isn't you. Talk to me, I beg you!"

"He's gone. He's out of our lives; leave me alone. I need to get high!"

She ran over to him and took the drugs from his hand. He didn't retaliate. She ripped open the bag and shook the contents into the toilet and flushed. He dropped to the floor with his head in his hands as she paced the bathroom floor.

"Why did he say you chose me? Is that what you were discussing out there, whether or not you wanted me?"

"You don't understand; you'll never understand."

"Try me. Sophie was right about you; you did try to seduce her husband. You made a pass at Rashid with me upstairs. A man, Daniel? Oh my God, you had drugs in our suite; you kept drugs in a hotel suite in Dubai, and you made a pass at a police officer!"

She was becoming hysterical; in a rage of fury, she threw her clothes into a bag and called a cab. At first, he didn't try to stop her. It was only after the cab sounded his horn outside that he got up from the bathroom floor to try and stop her.

"Please don't go. I can explain; please, I beg you. Don't leave me tonight."

"I don't know you anymore. I don't know who you are. You put our lives in serious danger. I understand now; I know you had a relationship with that man. I could live with that, but I can't live with the fear that you have more feeling for him than you do for me."

She broke down into tears, and he followed her to the waiting cab. As she climbed inside, he begged her one last time not to leave.

She opened the window and pointed to Harrison's room, saying, "Go to him. He's the one you want to be with."

As her cab pulled away, he noticed other guests were congregating outside Harrison's door. The hotel porter ran past him with a passkey in his hand; he was running to open Harrison's door. Daniel knew something was seriously wrong; as the porter opened the door, the other guests who looked inside started to scream. The porter quickly closed the door and called the emergency services. A lady who'd seen inside was crying hysterically; he could hear her telling the other guests who were comforting her what she'd seen: "That poor boy; blood, there's blood splattered everywhere. He's blown his brains out."

CHAPTER 9

A New Low

Daniel calmly turned to go inside. The junkie couple next door walked out to see what was going on. Before he opened the door, he asked the girl if she could help him.

He quickly ran inside to fetch a bundle of $20 bills and handed it to the guy, saying, "Please, I need your help. I need to get high!"

"You for real? Any minute now, this place will be crawling with cops," he said whilst counting the bundle of dollars; he thought for a moment and whispered into his girl's ear. "Karen will take you on a trip; how far do you wanna go?"

"As far as physically possible," Daniel said whilst rubbing his head, now starting to panic.

Karen took Daniel by the hand and walked him to the sidewalk in front of the hotel. Suddenly, a convoy of emergency vehicles screamed past them. The souped-up Chrysler soon pulled up to collect them. Inside the car, Karen held Daniel's hand as stared out of the window.

She said, "I always wanted to see America. I always wanted to travel."

"Ever since I was a small boy, I wanted to see real life. I guess this is real life."

Karen gripped him with her delicate cold hand and told him, "I'll help you travel, honey. Karen will take you to wherever you want to be."

After a ten-minute ride, they pulled up to a derelict house in the Southport area; the driver led the way to ensure that nobody was inside. They both knew the house well. Karen led Daniel to the bedroom, whilst the driver went into the kitchen to get a beer. Daniel switched on the TV at the bottom of the bed and searched for a news channel. He lay back and watched today's live news story unfold.

"Billionaire Shipping Tycoon's Son Suicide. Live from Indianapolis. Troubled Son."

It was only when he saw the stretcher carrying the body bag out of room 102 that it all became real.

"Did you know him?" Karen asked.

"Yes, I knew him. He wanted me; he wanted me so bad that after I rejected him, he raped me. I secretly adored him. I think I was in love with him."

"Yeah, yeah, honey, I believe you. We need to get on with this; I'm having dinner with Barack Obama."

He watched impatiently, with hunger in his eyes, as she heated a substance in foil over a candlelit flame. He craved being somewhere, anywhere, away from the hurt he now felt. He watched, intrigued, as she inserted a needle into a small piece of cotton soaking inside the foil to suck up the liquid substance. She tied the belt tight around his upper arm and told him to grip his fist tightly.

"It won't hurt, honey. I just need to find a vein."

"I'm a millionaire, Karen. There are so many things I want to do with my life. I want to own a big house by the sea. I want to learn how to windsurf."

"I'm sure you do; you'll soon be able to surf in the clouds, my sweet boy," she said as she inserted the needle in a vein. "Night-night, honey, sleep tight."

Almost immediately, he gasped as his body submerged into a warm luxurious tub and moaned a sigh of relief. The tension, the pain and the hurt fled his body and soul. He began to slowly rise from the tub and float up towards the ceiling. Karen was smiling from below; she waved him goodbye, just before his weightless body disappeared through the roof. The sky outside was dark; the higher he went, the lighter it became. He then floated above the soft white clouds with bright sunshine warming his body.

At his home in Middleton, Manchester, his mother Judith lay awake in bed after a sleepless night. She rarely called him on his mobile, but tonight was different. She was desperate to talk to him. She hadn't heard from him in days and was beginning to worry. She tried calling him throughout the night, but he never answered, She even called Emma in the early hours to ask if he'd been in touch with her; as a last resort, she called May.

Whilst awake, she watched a news channel covering the suicide of the son to a shipping tycoon and model/actress. She remembered Eva Fisher back in the early '90s at the height of her career; she recalled because her late husband was obsessed with her. Graham adored her; he thought she was the most beautiful woman that had ever set foot on this planet. He used to joke that if he was ever granted a free pass on their marriage, she'd be the lady. Judith's thoughts were with Eva tonight, losing a son in such tragic circumstances; he was the same age as her son.

It was midnight in Long Island. Eva was looking through photographs of Harrison's vacation to Thailand; she never got around to seeing them before. Her husband Billy was sipping whisky on a nearby sofa; their two youngest boys were asleep under a duvet next to him. Patiently, he waited for her to understand her loss. She pointed at a photograph of Harrison, Daniel, Lucas, and Ryan on a boat trip.

"Is this the boy, the one standing next to him? Is this the boy that came to your office with those accusations?"

With his glass in hand he walked over to see the photograph and said, "Yes, that's him. He's English; Parker already told me what Harrison had done to him. I hoped he'd have just stayed away."

With a tear falling from her eye, Eva zoomed in to look at the photograph closer; she said, "They look happy together; look how they're grinning at each other! Like they're sharing a joke that nobody else's was in on. Where is the boy now?"

"I believe he's staying at the same hotel."

"Well, did you ask the cops to question him? Surely he could help explain why he did it."

"No, you know damn well why I didn't. He gave his word he'd never speak about Harrison or what he did to him. I didn't want the cops to put any pressure on him; we don't need that being dragged up. Think about Mason and Gilles; they worshiped him. Damn it, they looked up to him. I don't want them to remember him for that!"

Eva walked out onto the dark beach; she stopped and stared out to sea. Billy watched from inside as she dropped to the sand, crying, and screamed.

Judith tried to call Daniel one last time. Karen was sitting in the passenger seat of her boyfriend Chad's car; she's holding his mobile. She could see it was his mum calling. Chad was counting what money was remained in his wallet.

"It's his mom, that poor boy. He's a good kid. I need to go back. I can't leave him like this. I'll need to leave him his cell phone!"

Chad, who was impatient to get away, started the engine. Karen's conscience got the better of her, and as the car was pulling away, she jumped out and ran back into the house. Chad angrily shouted abuse at her from the window and drove off without her.

Daniel continued to surf on the clouds for what seemed like an eternity. The bright sunshine was now fading, and it got cold. He closed his eyes and prepared himself for landing; whilst falling, he circled and spun out of control. The feeling of dizziness forced him to vomit; suddenly, he felt a sharp thumping on his back. At first, he thought it was the impact of hitting the bed, until he opened his eyes. Karen was now sitting on the bed, smiling at him.

"You made it back, honey; you were choking on your vomit. I hope I didn't hit you too hard."

He gazed at her with a blank expression, not knowing where he was or how he got here. She went to fetch him a towel to clean up his face. When she returned, he was staring, transfixed by the morning sunlight shining through the cracks in the boarded-up windows.

"He tried to take your wallet, Chad, that punk, the guy I'm screwing. He's a thieving low-life skank. Here, I wouldn't let him take your cell phone; your mom's been calling you through the night. You better call her back. I'll call us a cab back to Beech Lodge. Chad'll have checked out by now. can I use your room to freshen up?"

He looked at the phone and murmured, "Mum ... 11 missed calls. May ... two missed calls." Suddenly, his memories of yesterday came flooding back; he curled himself up into the foetal position and cried.

As they stepped out from the house, children were quieting on the sidewalk waiting for their school bus. As they walked past them on their way to the waiting cab, the children stared fearfully at him and Karen. The children had been warned about what takes place in that run-down house; they knew it was a drug den. Seeing two real-life junkies was somewhat of a novelty. To Karen, this was not uncommon to be stared at and looked down upon. But Daniel was mortified.

When they arrive back at Beech Lodge, May was sitting in a chair, waiting for his return. She looked at him with disgust as Karen followed him in. She knew what he'd been doing last night by the bruises on his arm. Suddenly, she leapt from out of the chair and screamed at Karen, "Get out, get the hell out of here!"

Furious, she dragged her by the hair back through the door.

Daniel yelled at her, "What the hell are you doing? She saved my life. Where the hell were you when I needed you most?"

"She saved your life, you say; I bet she did! You're worth more alive to her than dead; she'd have got you hooked and bled you dry. I came back here last night when I heard what had happened to your friend. I came back thinking you'd need me. Judging by your arm, you've taken heroin, and you spent the night with that whore. You disgust me!"

Daniel said, "You have no idea what I've been through over the last few months."

"No, Daniel, I don't. I have no idea because you never gave me the chance to understand. I know what happened to you. I know you were drugged and sexually abused in Samui. My mother told me, but she never told me who was responsible. I had to work that out for myself. She never betrayed your trust; she was too far gone on morphine. It's Harrison, the same one whose eyes you were staring lovingly into yesterday. The same person you care about more than you do me. I waited for you to tell me what had happened to you. I thought we were in love. I thought we'd never keep secrets from each other. Instead of talking to me, you went on a mission of self-destruction. I always knew you liked men as well as women. Auguste told me in Bangkok. It was never a problem; your lies are. Also, your mother called me last night; she was worried about you. I couldn't tell her where you were, because I didn't know. We had a good talk; why did you lie to me about your job?"

"I wanted to impress you. I didn't want you to think I was a nobody!"

"I never thought that. I fell for you before you started lying to me. You know something? This doesn't have to be the end. Apparently, I've got seven brothers and sisters in the UK. I have a British passport and wouldn't need a visa. Let's fly back to the UK. I'll get a job; it doesn't have to be in England, anywhere in Europe, Spain, France. We could get a home together, maybe children one day? Call the garage and ask them if they'd buy that ridiculous car of yours."

Daniel thought for a moment, his brain still confused and drained from last night; finally, he said, "Yes, yes, I'll come."

Whilst taking a bath, his head submerged under the water, he searched for answers in his addled mind. Perhaps May was right; maybe it was time to return home. However hard he tried, he couldn't remove Harrison from his mind; as much as he tried, he couldn't remove the pain and loneliness he now felt.

As his head emerged from the water, May was sitting on the bathtub, staring lovingly at him. She reached into the water to hold his hand.

"Everything will be fine, you'll see. Daniel, there's something I need to tell you. When you get home, I'd like you to see a doctor. I'm concerned about your mental state. I'd like you to get some counselling. I'd also like you to have a blood test."

Daniel released his hand from hers and furiously climbed out to dry himself down. "Blood test, counselling?"

"Yes. Please calm down, you know why. Harrison, that fiend that molested you, and last night, that whore who injected you with heroin. We ... I'm sorry, I meant I, believe it's the right thing to do."

"For your information, that friend used a condom and that whore used a clean new needle."

"You're spiralling into a world of substance abuse and alcohol dependency. Can't you see? This is how you became vulnerable to his abuse in the first place. I assume you were taking drugs the night he penetrated you? Now he's dead; there's no excuse not to get on with your life. I don't want to be part of your self-induced crisis; this is why you need counselling."

He shook his head in disbelief. He couldn't believe her naivety; he didn't bother to explain the facts. Without responding, he quickly got dressed and went outside to make a phone call.

On his return, he looked furious. He grabbed her by the neck and pushed her up against a bureau.

"I've just spoken to my mother," he spat. "She said she's looking forward to meeting you. She can't wait to have me home. She also said she'll be happy when I'm back in the UK, where it's safe and where I can seek help. Tell me, what did she mean by that? What did you tell my mother?"

With his hand around her throat, she struggled to talk. She raised both hands and managed to prise his hand away.

"I'm sorry, she mentioned what she'd seen on the news. She knew we were staying close to where he shot himself. She could hear hesitation in my voice. She begged, she pleaded with me; you have to believe me. I couldn't lie to her. I had to tell her."

He took another firm grip of her throat again and snarled, "You told her everything, didn't you? You stupid, controlling, interfering, condescending bitch. Didn't you even stop for a moment and consider my pride and dignity? What gave you the right to discuss something so personal behind my back, and to my mother? Damn you, I feel violated, ashamed, a victim all over again. So help me God, I've never been so close to hitting you."

Like a rabid dog foaming at the mouth, he looked into her eyes as if he were about to kill her. He drew back his fist, tightened his lips, and punched the mirror behind her. He loosened his grip as the shards of glass fell around her feet and calmly wrapped a pillowcase cover around his cut knuckles. She sat on the bed, massaging her neck; in tears, she watched fearfully as he walked to the door.

"I'm going out to get drunk," he said. "I'll be out for some time. When I return, I'll expect you not to be here."

"Daniel, you have to realise: I only told her because I care for you. I just want you to be that same person again, that same person I fell in love with in Bangkok."

He turned to her one last time; his anger was now subsiding. He said sadly, "May, I'll never be that person again. You have money; you'll have a better life without me!"

He spent the day drinking in downtown Indianapolis. He thought this to be a more sensible idea than his first option. That option was to take heroin again; his head was in turmoil with feelings of anger, grief, regret, and guilt. He was desperate to eliminate these feelings. When the alcohol kicked in, for a short time, he almost managed to convince himself he was enjoying his newfound freedom. But as the day went on, drinking alone, he stared at people laughing and enjoying their lives; he felt isolated and damaged.

He arrived back at the hotel the room to find it cleaned and the mirror replaced. He noticed a pile of neatly folded clothes on the dresser; they were all the clothes he'd bought for May. On the top was the Versace dress he'd bought for her in Dubai; next to the pile was a handwritten note with her engagement ring.

Dear Daniel

Your love for me and your generosity towards my family was never taken for granted. I will say a prayer for you every night and I hope that you find true happiness within yourself.

With all my love

May

He could still smell her perfume on the dress; he lay with it in his arms on the bed and cried himself to sleep. He only slept for an hour; he was rudely woken by the hotel manager, knocking loudly at his door. He wanted to discuss the repair bill for the broken mirror. After Daniel handed over $175 cash to replace it, the manager looked suspiciously around room.

"Will there be anything else?" Daniel asked, hoping he'd leave soon.

"Listen, son, I don't care what kids do within these four walls, but if I suspect any punks dealing shit from Beech Lodge, I come down on them like a ton of lead, you hear me?"

Daniel looked puzzled and asked, "Why would you think I take drugs, let alone sell them?"

He turned and walked to door, saying, "I'll bid you farewell and leave you in peace. Enjoy your stay, son; just remember what I said."

After he left, he paced up and down the room, wishing he was sober and had his car so he could drive away from this hellhole. He turned the TV on and played music to try and drown out the feelings of loneliness and isolation. There was only one escape from this tonight, and that was to drink more alcohol. He bought a large bottle of citrus vodka tonic water from the nearby drinks store. He lay on the bed, drinking and looking through photographs on his MacBook.

As the hours passed, he became more and more depressed. Judith tried to call him, but he didn't answer. He was scared of what he might say to her or what she might ask. As far as he was concerned, she was as much to blame as May, for blabbing personal information. She stopped calling and sent an email, begging him to answer her calls. He knew May had spoken to her again and feared what she'd told her this time.

Somebody was knocking at the door again; he didn't answer it. He wanted to be left alone, to wallow in self-pity. The knocking stopped; he got off the bed to peek through the curtains and see who was there. His legs collapsed before him, and he fell to floor at the bottom of the bed. Paralytic, he struggled to get up. Lying on the carpet, he noticed a shard of broken mirror hidden in between the bureau and dresser. He reached for it and looked his reflection; he was repulsed by what he saw. Gently, with very little pressure, he glided the sharpest edge across his wrist. The cut wasn't deep, yet just enough to draw blood. He felt a sense of relief that the pain would finally stop. As the blood trickled onto the carpet, he could hear voices from outside his room. It sounded like two men arguing.

He lay face down, with his chin resting on the floor; suddenly, he heard the door open. His vision was impaired, and he struggled to keep his eyes open. He could just make out somebody wearing boots slowly walking to where he was lying. He reached out his bloodstained hand and tried to grab the leg of the stranger for help. His eyes closed, too weak to stay open. Everything went dark and silent.

With his eyes still closed, he woke to the sound of country music coming from the radio. Fearful of what mess he'd made last night, he slowly opened one eye at a time. The room looked tidy; his wrist had been neatly dressed and bandaged. Even the blood stain on the carpet had been cleaned. There was nobody else in the room, but he could see a small suitcase on the chair and could smell freshly sprayed deodorant coming from the bathroom. He rested his head back down on the pillow. It was too painful to get out of bed. There wasn't a part of his body that didn't ache. Suddenly, the door began to open; it was Richard.

Daniel stared in disbelief at him. He stuttered, "You ... what ... how?"

Richard was carrying two takeout breakfasts; he closed the door behind him and looked at Daniel, more surprised than he was.

"Get out of here! You don't remember? Jeez, you sure was wasted! I told you why I was here last night. After I dressed your wound, we talked. Well, you slurred, I listened. You told me everything; after we made out, you promised me that million dollars Fisher paid you to keep your mouth shut. You said you didn't want his dirty cash!"

Daniel, shocked by this, looked under the duvet to see what he was wearing. Richard handed him his breakfast and laughed, saying, "Here, butthead, you need to eat. I might have exaggerated on the making out and the money. Hey, you can't fault me for trying."

He tucked into his breakfast like he'd not eaten in years. Richard ate his whilst he passed around the room, talking: "When you're done, you gonna drag that sorry ass out bed and get washed? No offence, boy, but you look like shit and stink of liquor. Hope you don't mind, but I took it upon myself to answer your cell phone. You were still out of it when they called. It was Blake's Autos; they left a message saying your car's ready."

Daniel made himself comfortable under the duvet; he wasn't ready to face the world, and besides, he was in no fit state to drive. He begged Richard to collect his car on his behalf. He suggested he'd pay by card over the phone and give authority for him to collect it. Richard agreed, on the condition that he was washed, dressed, and ready to face the world when he returned.

Two hours later, when he returned with the car, Daniel was still unwashed and lying in bed. Richard furiously dragged him from his bed and forced him into the bathroom. Daniel stood holding onto the sink, trying to support his weak, trembling body. He turned to Richard and pleaded for him to leave him alone.

Richard stormed in and yelled, "You want me to leave you alone? You think I'm gonna just walk outta here? Hey, if I leave you alone, you'll leave here in a body bag, like that Fisher boy. I ain't gonna let that happen."

Tearfully, he pushed Richard out of the bathroom and locked the door. He knew he was right; he sat on the toilet with his head in his hands.

Richard continued to shout through the door, "That Fisher kid is lying on a slab in some morgue. What do you think his parents are going through right now? It's Wednesday now. I don't need to be back in Miami until Friday. How about you come with me? I live in a big old house; it gets lonely sometimes. I'll drive: it'll give me a chance to enjoy that beast of yours. If we leave pretty soon, we could get to Nashville come sunset. What do you say, boy?"

Daniel was still sitting on the toilet, unwrapping his bandage, terrified to see what harm he'd done to himself. He breathed a sigh of relief when he saw the shallow cut, knowing it would heal without any medical treatment. From that moment on, he swore he'd never let himself get this low again. He knew he must leave the hotel. Richard was pacing around the room, waiting for his answer. He was holding his mobile, checking to see who'd called him. The person who'd called him twice before phoned again; he quickly switched to silent mode, not wanting to talk to that person. Daniel suddenly appeared at the bathroom door holding up his wrist; he smiled and thanked him for dressing his wound.

"Well, are you coming with me?" Richard asked.

The prospect of returning home a failure, a victim, damaged, and heartbroken after yet another disastrous relationship terrified him. Although he hardly knew this person who mysteriously turned up at his time of need, he was unsure of his motives. The one thing he knew for sure was that this was his only chance for survival, to save him from himself; the answer was a definite yes.

With Richard at the wheel, Daniel made himself comfortable in the passenger seat, ready for the journey. Richard reached into his pocket for his mobile, to see who was calling him again. Eva Fisher's name flashed up on the screen. He quickly jumped out of the car to answer the call in private, away from Daniel. He pressed Answer and held the phone against his ear, saying, "Carlos? Carlos is that you? Are you there? Please talk to me."

He didn't reply; a tear formed in his eye. He wiped away the tear and replied, "I'm here."

"We need to talk. We need to talk about our boy. We need to talk about Harrison," she said emotionally.

"So now, you want to talk. It's a bit late to discuss our child. I have to go. I can't talk just now."

When Richard returned to the car, Daniel was staring transfixed at the room where Harrison shot himself. He looked fragile, gaunt, and terrified, trembling like a young child who'd insisted on watching a horror movie, only to regret it.

He turned to Richard and said, "Take me away; drive off. We need to leave now. Take me to a place where I have no feelings, no remorse, no guilt, and no emotions."

ABOUT THE AUTHOR

Stephen Buckley had a happy, loving upbringing in North Wales, where he still lives to this day. He never knew what his true vocation in life was. After working various unskilled jobs, he decided to follow his dreams of being either a chef or an architect. His creative and constrictive mind led him to study architecture; unfortunately, his university of choice was Brighton, a glamorous city known for being vibrant, bohemian, creative, liberated, exotic, and cultural. Sadly, his love for Brighton overtook his enthusiasm to study. This left him wishing he'd trained to be the next Jamie Oliver in a less glamorous city in Northern England. Buckley now works as a long-distance driver. Driving for long periods of time helps him to imagine and create fascinating characters and stories. Nothing gives him greater pleasure than reading a story or watching a movie that makes him cry with laughter or moves him to tears. After a hectic week on the road, nothing makes him happier than returning home to his sleepy village in the Welsh mountains, where his long-term partner, a beautiful black Labrador named Brando, is waiting for him.

ABOUT THE BOOK

On the day Daniel Reed inherited money from his late father's estate, his long-term girlfriend, Emma, told him she was pregnant with his child. This came as a complete surprise, especially when they'd planned to travel the world together. What came as more of a surprise is that Emma also confessed to having an affair with his best friend. Heartbroken, vulnerable, and confused about his sexuality, Daniel sets off to travel the world by himself in an attempt to meet fascinating new people and perhaps a new love interest.

Surfing on a Cloud is a tale of adventure, love, and exploration; it explores complex relationships, painful realisations, and deep revelations – a journey of self-discovery. Every emotion is covered within this story: love and lust, happiness and hatred, despair and sorrow.

Surfing on a Cloud creates a web of interesting lives, spanning the globe with unexpected surprises. The reader will empathise with Daniel as he travels to beautiful destinations and struggles with emotions that tear him apart.

With good looks, money, and charm, Daniel meets the girl of his dreams in Thailand. What could possibly go wrong?

CPSIA information can be obtained
at www.ICGtesting.com
Printed in the USA
FFOW04n1111050217
32093FF